I0718647

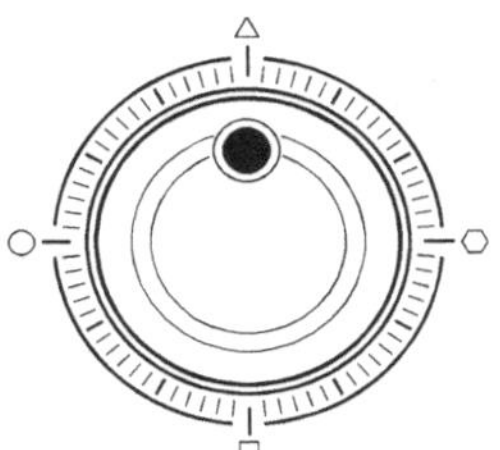

THE CHARGE
OF THE
WOLVERHINO

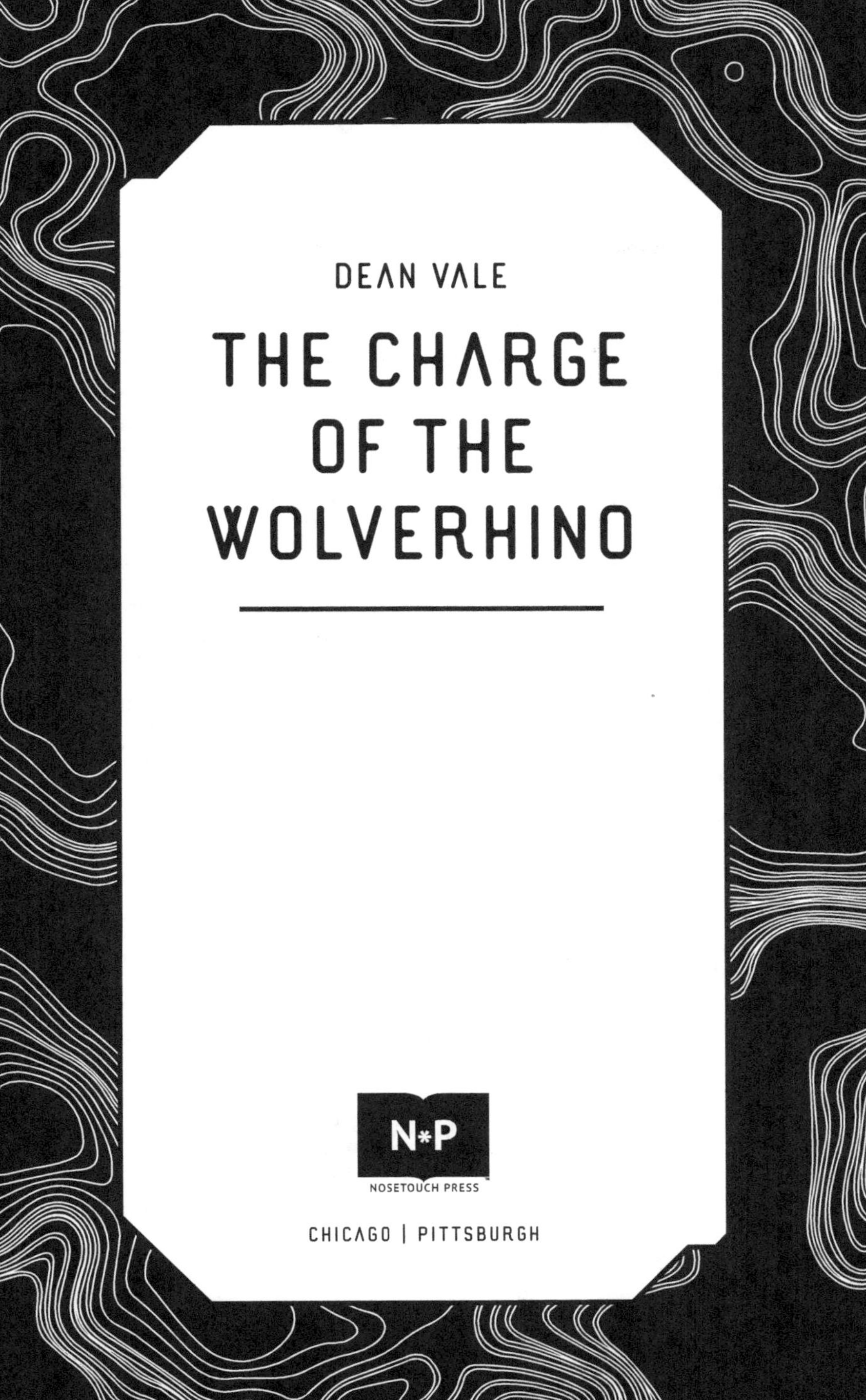

DEAN VALE

THE CHARGE OF THE WOLVERHINO

NOSETOUCH PRESS

CHICAGO | PITTSBURGH

The Charge of the Wolverhino
© 2021 by Dean Vale. All Rights Reserved.

ISBN-13: 978-1-944286-17-0

Published by Nosetouch Press
www.nosetouchpress.com

For more information about bulk purchases,
please contact Nosetouch Press at info@nosetouchpress.com.

Cataloging-in-Publication Data

Names: Vale, Dean., author.
Title: The Charge of the Wolverhino / Dean Vale
Description: Chicago, IL : Nosetouch Press [2021]
Identifiers: ISBN: 9781944286170 (paperback)
Subjects: LCSH: Science—Fiction. | GSAFD: Science fiction. |
BISAC: FICTION / Science Fiction / Genetic Engineering.

Cover & interior designed by
Christine M. Scott, Clever Crow Consulting and Design
www.clevercrow.com

The text for this book was set in Minion Pro.

For Key, one you'll be happy to unlock one day.

THE OFFER

"Let me see it," Felix Jaeger asked the Gaiacon rep, Sloane Ketteridge. She pulled up the files on her tablet and slid it across the table for him to see. She was conventionally pretty, with honey blonde hair and seemingly deliberately geeky black-rimmed glasses over her big grey eyes. That bookish look contrasted with the sleek, royal blue dress she wore. Gaiacon's patented corporate color, that royal blue. She wore the Gaiacon logo brooch pinned near her neck. It was a Mercator globe disc with latitude and longitude lines, and what looked like a crescent-shaped bite taken out of it.

Jaeger himself was tall and tanned, middle-aged but militarily fit, wearing an ivory suit with a cream-colored, ribbed mock turtleneck. He wore a chunky silver signet ring on his pinky finger, upon which was a lion rampant, rendered in lapis. He kept his greying hair slightly longer than it needed to be, giving him the bearing of a lapsed aristocrat.

Ms. Ketteridge had visited him in his French Colonial home in Montreal, and he'd received her in his trophy room, festooned with the antlers, horns, tusks and heads of all of the game he'd taken in his heyday. They were all perfectly preserved and meticulously free of dust, despite some of them having been taken 20 years earlier.

"The Wolverhino is Gaiacon's new flagship product," Sloane said. "We're revitalizing big-game hunting with this novel species: The Wolverhino is unrelentingly savage, with a brutally aggressive disposition that is sure to please even the most discriminating big game hunters."

Gaiacon had approached Jaeger with an offer of 500,000 in Gaiacoin (GC) if he was able to successfully bring down their Wolverhino.

As one of the last big game hunters still living before most of the remaining big game species had gone extinct in the wild, Jaeger had won both acclaim and infamy for his tenacious, old-school stalking approach to hunting.

In past years, he had been vocal in both his support for big game hunting and for the conservation of wilderness, but the dismal tide of the Anthropecene Extinction had been too great, and big game hunting nearly went out with the rest of the big game in the wild.

That's when Gaiacon had apparently stepped in. The company's biotech division had set itself to the task of "solving" the "problem" of the absence of credible big game to match the classic Fatal Five of hunting lore: lion, African elephant, leopard, rhino, and Cape buffalo. The truly dangerous game that could kill a careless hunter.

Jaeger studied the three-dimensional display of the beast Gaiacon had created through proprietary genetic engineering. The creature was a hulking specimen, with a ghastly face, keeping the general rhinoceros shape but with a far more muscular body, and a luxuriantly thick brown coat that bore marvelous grey countershading, two lighter-brown streaks on either side of it, coming together at the thing's toothy muzzle.

"It looks sort of like a monstrous woolly rhino," Jaeger said, making Sloane smile. Her smile was coolly welcoming, conspiratorial without being comradely.

Gaiacon had already made a name for themselves by bringing back the woolly mammoth, the mastodon, and the woolly rhinoceros. But those efforts, drawing from exposed remains of prehistoric mammals pulled from the melting permafrost, had been largely PR exercises, and were currently off-limits to hunters. They had, however, shown what Gaiacon was capable of, in the realm of genetics.

"Yes," she said. "Our gene samplers took the most useful traits from the white, black, Indian, Javan, and Sumatran rhinoceros species genomes we had on file and blended them to create a splendid new animal. The Wolverhino bull you see there weighs around 4000 kilograms and has a shoulder height of three meters, an overall length of six meters. Its horn reaches 1.5 meters."

In his brain, he did the conversions from the more clinical metric—nearly 9,000 pounds, over seven feet at the shoulder, and 20 feet long, with a horn of five feet in length. Jaeger whistled, could only imagine how that would look on the wall of his trophy room, was already mentally rearranging things to accommodate it. The thing would need its own display room.

"Begging your pardon, but why would you even splice in the wolverine DNA?" he asked.

"Great question," Sloane said. "Simply put, we wanted to push the boundaries of big game hunting into areas that had never been before. We could have simply brought back the rhino, but you know how overdeveloped Africa's become these days. And I'm sure you know about our Nextinction campaign with the mammoth and other prehistoric animals. The public just loves those animals. We can't bring them back only to have hunters kill them."

She paused a moment, looking at Jaeger down the end of her perfect nose, before continuing. Jaeger had watched the mammoths and woolly rhinos on trideo, had wished they'd let him hunt them, but Gaiacon had taken a very high-minded stance against it, speaking of the need for conservation and giving these species a second chance. It had been a PR masterstroke, as Jaeger saw it. Gaiacon, the Company that Cared™.

"For us, it was a case of wanting to bring something new to the table. You yourself know what big business big game hunting can be. Gaiacon wanted to corner that market with our 'Prey for the Future' campaign. Hunters already knew how to hunt rhino, and between poachers and hunters, hunted them into extinction. But the Wolverhino? That's another thing entirely. 'Game Changers' is what Marketing calls our Gaiacon gene sequencing initiative. We are changing the game, Mr. Jaeger."

Sloane slid a finger across her presentation tablet and showed a schematic putting a 1.8 meter tall man next to the Wolverhino computer display. The man's head didn't even reach the thing's shoulder.

"It can run over 72 kilometers per hour," Sloane said. "It has over 15 centimeter-long claws that can tear through plate steel like paper. It's nearly tireless and is ferociously aggressive. It has great hearing and an even better sense of smell. Poor eyesight is baked into the design, but that just magnifies its aggressive, territorial behavior, and is more than offset by the other senses. The Wolverhino will attack anything that gets too close to it, and it will not stop until the intruder is dead. It is entirely without fear."

She flicked the display and watched the digital Wolverhino trotting, moving in that light-stepped way that rhinos had that belied their considerable size, but with a side-to-side shamble that called to mind the wolverine as well. It was monstrous to behold, even on the digital display.

"What does it eat?" Jaeger asked.

"It's omnivorous," Sloane said. "It is a general ruminant that is also an opportunistic predator and gifted scavenger. By making it an omnivore, we felt it would boost its survival chances in the wild."

"So, it can hunt?" Jaeger said.

"Oh, yes," Sloane said, showing the Wolverhino bringing down a fanged Siberian musk deer with a swipe of its monstrous horn, and feeding on the savaged corpse. The image dissolved into a shot of the Wolverhino chasing off a Siberian tiger, charging after the frightened big cat.

"We've engineered the Wolverhino for snowfari expeditions, in areas where there is still some snow to be found—so, we're already talking about remote locations, like Siberia, for instance."

"I see," Jaeger said "And Russia doesn't mind?"

Sloane pushed her glasses up her perfect nose. "We've made the necessary arrangements with the

Russians. We have kilometers of forest purchased expressly for the purpose of this test."

"Why would Gaiacon want me to kill their prize specimen?" Jaeger asked. Not that he minded the prize they offered him for the hunt. He just could not imagine a company wanting to risk losing a prototype chimera they had spent so much money and time developing.

"If you'll forgive me, Mr. Jaeger," Sloane said. "It's because Gaiacon believes that you won't succeed in killing the Wolverhino. We wanted to test it against one of the best remaining big game hunters out there."

Jaeger smirked at the young woman, who leaned forward in her seat, one smooth leg crossed over the other. They regarded one another in silence. Jaeger could not be sure in that moment which of them was the predator, and which was the prey.

"You're asking me to wager my life," Jaeger said. "For only 500,000 GC."

"Yes," Sloane said. "But you'll be the first man in history to have successfully hunted and killed a Wolverhino."

"Or the first to be killed by one," Jaeger said.

"Not the first, sadly," Sloane said. "The Wolverhino has already managed an impressive kill count among Gaiacon field-testing personnel when it had been released at the Siberian facility. And, if you accept our deal, you'll be the third big game hunter we've sent against it."

Jaeger felt a sense of wounded pride that he was their third choice.

"Who else went against it?" he asked.

"Christoph Jilton," Sloane said. "And Roland Abercrombie."

Jaeger nodded, knew both of them well, although they had never crossed paths in their time as hunters. Their reputations as big game hunters were nearly as great as his own.

"And it killed both of them?" Jaeger asked. He admitted to himself that he'd glossed over the stories about their deaths, but remembered that the news stories were not noteworthy—Abercrombie supposedly died in a plane crash, while Jilton had suffered an untimely heart attack that led to a fatal car accident. Clearly, Gaiacon hadn't wanted their pet monster getting that kind of publicity just yet. "Your company covered up their deaths, then."

"We didn't want there to be any unnecessary and distracting coverage getting out there about the Wolverhino. People can be so easily triggered," Sloane said. "So, we mediated the situation and provided discreet-yet-ample compensation to the families of the hunters contingent on their keeping silent about the specifics of the deaths of Jilton and Abercrombie. As we saw it, the families didn't need to know exactly how they died, only that they died in accidents. We didn't want any bad press souring the project."

"Of course not," Jaeger said. "Can't have that."

Sloane nodded, touching her tablet and showing the mangled remains of both Jilton and Abercrombie, also in three-dimensional display, which she helpfully turned with her clear-lacquered and meticulously manicured fingernails.

The men had been torn apart and half-eaten, by the look of them. Savaged. Jaeger was used to death, and was unfazed by it. But, on an objective, analytical level, both men had clearly been overmatched by this Wolverhino. Jaeger knew them both to be superb hunters. That they'd been taken by the creature spoke volumes about its lethality.

"Since you'd been semi-retired, Mr. Jaeger, we did not approach you initially with this opportunity," Sloane said. She was covering her bases, already, he thought, with some bemusement.

"I only retired because I ran out of worthy prey to hunt," Jaeger said, gesturing to the trophies around them. "It's not my fault, but, rather, the fault of the world. Or what we're doing to it, at any rate. Plus, my Tilda wanted me to quit."

He glanced at the picture of his late wife, who looked out at them in the holographic portrait like a ghost. She smiled at them with aged radiance, as he'd had the portrait made in the last decade they'd shared together. A handsome woman with strong features and white hair that hung in a ponytail, one stray lock swaying in the hologram. Her tanned skin and blue eyes would follow him when he crossed the room.

Sloane turned her own gaze to the portrait, nodding solemnly. According to the Gaiacon files, Tilda had died five years ago of a tropical hemorrhagic fever, which she'd caught in Latin America, on one of her charitable outings. Tilda Jaeger had been very active in the conservation movement, and her loss was keenly felt in that community. Jaeger had formed the Tilda Foundation in her honor, dedicated to the conservation of the remaining wildlife and wild spaces left in the world.

"We completely understand, Mr. Jaeger," Sloane said. "And if you don't feel up to the task, we've already got Lester Kishwalla lined up as our next prospective hunter."

"Kishwalla?" Jaeger said. "Please. That man has no finesse whatsoever. He hunts giraffes with assault rifles, for god's sake. That's brutality and sadism, not good sport."

"Precisely," Sloane said. "But that's where we'll go if you prove uninterested."

Jaeger looked the young woman up and down. He studied her contours, the details of her assiduously gym-toned frame. He studied her steady, calm breathing, and knew that she was baiting him. The young Ms. Ketteridge clearly knew how to manage big game hunters. He wondered if Gaiacon taught special client management techniques for them, or whether it was just a well-tendered understanding of human foibles that they were able to apply in these situations. People remained people, regardless of technological or cultural advances. He decided to play her game, to see how it would end up.

"I didn't say I was uninterested," Jaeger said. "I'm just worth far more than 500,000 GC, you must understand."

Sloane accepted that with a tilt of her head. "Gaiacon is prepared to offer one million GC for the successful hunting of the Wolverhino. No higher, however. Even we have our limits."

"Is that how you negotiate?" Jaeger asked. "Doubling your prize?"

Sloane merely smiled at him thinly.

"You have no family," Sloane said. "No obligations. We value your skill. You can't fault us for coming in low."

"No, I suppose I can't," Jaeger said. "I know you have the money. Gaiacon stock has skyrocketed for the past decade."

"We've done very well," Sloane said. "Our investors are very pleased with our performance."

"I'm sure they are," Jaeger replied.

Jaeger considered it, mulled it over in his head, wondered about Jilton and Abercrombie, whether they'd been given the same offer, and what he could learn from them, if anything.

"Is there a time limit?" Jaeger asked. "Or am I free to hunt it as long as I like?"

Sloane's expression was one of practiced client relations tolerance.

"As long as it takes, Mr. Jaeger," she said.

"I won't be rushed," Jaeger said. "There's nothing less satisfying than a rushed hunt. I want to take my time to savor it."

She appeared to understand that, nodded.

"Of course, we want it to be an enjoyable hunt for you, Mr. Jaeger. I'll check in with you when I can, and at the end, to get your feedback. Assuming, of course, that you are not killed by our product."

"Yes, of course," Jaeger said. "Assuming I'm not torn to pieces."

Sloane adopted the most solicitous of expressions, her grey eyes widening into shallow pools of corporate compassion.

"We want only the best possible outcome for you, Mr. Jaeger," Sloane said. "As proud as we are of our

Wolverhino, the client matters most to us. We want it to provide a new and satisfying experience for elite hunters like yourself. Danger must, as you know, come into it. That's precisely what makes big game hunting what it is. If the Wolverhino is simply too dangerous a product, that poses problems for Gaiacon. We want it to be just dangerous enough, but not so lethal that nobody dares to hunt it. Trust me when I say that we're all pulling for you. An entire team and marketing campaign depends on your successful hunt, Mr. Jaeger."

Jaeger hardly believed a word of it, but not because she wasn't convincing. Rather, it was because Jaegar had lived long enough to be profoundly skeptical of corporate sincerity whenever he ran across it. Mission statements and corporate ethics boiled away in the brute force of the requirements of the market. Tilda jousted with them throughout her conservation efforts.

"There will always be someone willing to hunt it," Jaeger said.

"We're not talking about spoiled heirs driving around in armored cars equipped with .50 caliber machine guns, Mr. Jaeger," Sloane said. "We're talking about a better class of client."

"May I bring my Winchester?" he asked, referring to Beauty, his double-barreled Winchester Magnum .458, his very favorite hunting rifle. She hung over the fireplace, and he gestured toward her, drawing Sloane's eyes there. Her eyes took in Beauty in a moment, before darting back to him.

"You may use whatever weapon you like, Mr. Jaeger," Sloane said, glancing back at Beauty once more, before returning to him and lingering. "We have no restrictions on choice of weapon in this particular hunt. The Wolverhino's thick hide is impervious to small arms fire, we've found. I would not recommend bowhunting or spear-hunting in this instance."

Jaeger chuckled at that. Although he'd done some of that in his youth, it was certainly a young man's sort of hunting, not something he'd done in over twenty years, and not something he'd consider for the Wolverhino. Being a good hunter meant not being a fool, a coward, or a clown.

"Am I going to be alone?" Jaeger asked. "I like to stalk my prey, and I don't want anyone getting in my way."

"There'll be a driver and a cameraman to record it," Sloane said. "The driver is Landon James, and the cameraman is Samuel Henry. Both have been cleared by Gaiacon."

Jaeger tapped the table gently but decisively with an outstretched finger. "I don't want them interfering."

"They won't. They've been briefed on their roles on this expedition," Sloane said. "Believe me, Mr. Jaeger, we don't want anyone interfering on this hunt."

"And the true purpose of this hunt is what?"

Sloane smiled playfully at him. She had him right where she wanted him. Ms. Ketteridge was a solitary cat, he'd decided. An ambush predator, supremely confident in her approach. He could see why Gaiacon had entrusted this young woman to the task of bagging him.

"It's our third field test, Mr. Jaeger. We want to see if the Wolverhino gives good sport in the manner we intended. If it proves to be a good—that is, successful—hunt for you, then we'll push forward with full-blown marketing of the Wolverhino for our Siberian preserve, with opportunities to get it transported to northern Canada as well. Big game hunting's always going to remain a niche market. But it's a lucrative one we fully intend to capture with this project. Gaiacon does not like to see hunters without anything to hunt. The Wolverhino is just the beginning, I assure you, although I'm not at liberty to discuss our other product lines with you at this time. There may be other opportunities for you, should you survive."

"Why'd you pick those two species to blend?" Jaeger asked.

"Market research and testing, Mr. Jaeger. The rhino has, historically, always been one of the most satisfying, challenging, even frustrating of hunts," Sloane said. "And the wolverine is renowned for its unmatched ferocity and survival instinct. We wanted the best of both worlds."

She tapped the tablet with her perfect nails again and once again the digital Wolverhino filled the frame, the digitally-rendered beast snarling at the camera, the great horn on its nose waving as it charged.

"We mapped out the qualities of those source species and thought it was a perfect pairing," Sloane said. "And the name is catchy, you must admit."

"Yes, it's a wonderfully absurd name," Jaeger said. "Because Rhinorine, to be sure, which sounds more like an antiseptic nasal spray, or perhaps an antimalarial medication."

Sloane smiled politely through his little quip.

"Quite right, Mr. Jaeger," Sloane said. "The Wolverhino, on the other hand, well, it practically sells itself. For the right sort of client, obviously."

"Obviously. And if I successfully kill it," Jaeger said. "I'll get my million GC and will I get to keep the pelt and the head?"

"Naturally," Sloane said. "We want you to enjoy the complete experience, Mr. Jaeger. We want this to be worth your time. The pelt and head will be yours to keep, when this is all done. You'll be a celebrity, even more than you already are, within your circle. It's a rare thing for a hunter to go on the record as the first one to bring something down, and to be known around the world for it. Assuming, as I said before, you survive. Gaiacon will have your back on this. Think of what it would do to propel your conservation efforts, that kind of attention."

He'd already decided five minutes before, but kept his cool to get to the million that he wanted. Successful hunting, more often than not, meant making the right move at precisely the right time. This was that time.

—

THE EXPEDITION

THE THREE MEN HAD PACKED THEMSELVES INTO THE arctic Land Rover, reaching the perimeter of the Gaiacon Experimental Arctic Reserve (GEAR) from the private airstrip in record time. Since it was late fall, there was a slight snow on the ground, a thin crust and dusting of it on the seemingly endless expanse of taiga that unfolded before them in the distance. In some areas, the snow was even thickly fallen.

On the flight in, Jaeger had been poring over the files of Jilton and Abercrombie. Sloane had offered to share with him the videos clips they had of their ill-fated hunts, but Jaeger had turned that down.

"Really?" she asked. He admitted that he had only skimmed the files on his rivals, not wanting to know all of the gory details—not because he was squeamish, but because he didn't want to ruin the surprise of his encounter with the Wolverhino. He did not want his perception to be colored by the failure of the others.

"Absolutely," Jaeger said. "I want to approach this with my own eyes, ears, and instincts. Their last moments with the beast were their own. And, obviously, yours."

Ms. Ketteridge seemed amused by the sentiment, which showed on her face in the guise of the barest hint of a smile.

"Quite the romantic, you are, Mr. Jaeger," Sloane said.

"Clearly," Jaeger said. "Hunting and romanticism play very well together. Romantics are always hunting for something—what it is they are hunting for exactly, of course, depends on the person."

Her whisper of a smile didn't fade, as she watched him with her grey cat's eyes, as inscrutable as ever. She did not strike Jaeger as a romantic.

At the GEAR, Gaiacon's wardens and rangers looked at Jaeger's snowfari team with ashen faces that stood out against their royal blue parkas that bore Gaiacon globe patches. Behind them was a thick reinforced concrete wall topped with razorwire, which stretched as far as Jaeger could see—which wasn't very far, owing to the fog that hung out across the landscape.

"You're crazy to go in there, Mr. Jaeger," said Vitaly Ivanova, the chief ranger. He was a rough-hewn man in that soldierly way that so many Russian men carried about them—square-jawed, nearly shaved head, deep-set eyes, prominent nose, a face more cragged than wrinkled. His concern was all but carved on his face. "They sent those two other great hunters in there before, and we had to take them out in bins."

"I know," Jaeger said. "I saw the photographs, Mr. Ivanova. Thank you for your consideration."

"The Wolverhino is like nothing you have ever hunted," Ivanova said. "Savage, yet elusive. It keeps to itself, then comes at you like, I don't know what—

angry bear. Unbelievably hostile. Worse than anything."

"'Worse than anything?' I rather like the sound of that, Mr. Ivanova," Jaeger said. "If that's intended to deter me, you must know that it only spurs me on."

Ivanova seemed reconciled to the futility of his gesture, judging from the careworn look he carried with him.

"I know," he said. "But the others, they went in confident, too. They did not know what they were up against. Wolverhino is no joke. It will kill you, if you let it."

Jaeger looked at Ivanova with amusement.

"That's precisely the point, isn't it?" Jaeger asked. "It's a rare thing to face the unknown like this. Rarer still to be granted the opportunity to hunt a certifiable monster. And it is a monster, by the look of it."

"Yes," Ivanova said. "A monster."

"There you have it," Jaeger said. "I'm a monster hunter."

Ivanova nodded, held out a meaty hand.

"Need your cell phones," Ivanova said. "Company policy. No outside telecom in the GEAR."

"Of course," Jaeger said, handing over his phone. Sam Henry and Landon James did, too, which Ivanova put into a lockbox. He then handed it over to one of his lieutenants, cleared his throat.

"You need help, you call us on your radio," Ivanova said. "And you *will* need help."

"Will we?" Jaeger asked. "Let's get to it, then."

He gestured toward the thick gate. Ivanova spoke Russian into his radio, confirmed that the Wolverhino was not sighted anywhere nearby, and Ivanova pushed a button and opened it, the heavy doors swinging inward on powerful pneumatic hinges.

"Onward, Mr. James," Jaeger said. Landon gunned the electric engine and the Land Rover sped quietly through the gates, which closed behind them as soon as they'd passed, past the alert wardens with their assault rifles at the ready.

Jaeger was pleased to be on the hunting grounds at last. After his initial discussion with Ms. Ketteridge in Montreal, there had been a month of preparation on his part. During that time, he had studied files on the Wolverhino, Jilton, Abercrombie, the wolverine, and the rhino species. The notion of hunting a certifiable monster thrilled him beyond reckoning. Gaiacon's marketers may have been onto something with their Game Changer program, he admitted to himself.

The creation of tailor-made chimeras culled from noteworthy remaining species offered bountiful opportunities for hunts. It was both mad and madly brilliant, and it all hinged on his own success on this hunt.

He scanned the horizon, hoping for an early sighting of the Wolverhino, but there was no sign of it in the rolling grassland that gave way to bands of thick taiga.

"Wolverhino, he don't like visitors on his prop," James said. He was a 20-something, mush-mouthed Southern man out of Baton Rouge. He had longish, peat brown hair and forest green eyes, and had a dusty brown beard that made him look like a natural brigand who only needed shoreline to raid and cattle to steal.

Sam Henry, the photographer-cameraman, was an African-American man from Baltimore, had picked up a Russian-made ushanka somewhere which he had jammed down on his shaved head and just cocked his eyebrow at Jaeger. Henry had an angular, formidable face that spoke to a military background of some sort, likely Army, by Jaeger's estimation. Possibly Marines.

"I want to sneak a photo of it for Transnational Geographic," Henry said. "Gaiacon has been riding my ass about this. They don't want any publicity getting out that their marketing department hasn't approved. Not after what happened to the other fellows. And they're embargoing whatever I shoot until they've had time to review."

Jaeger glanced at Henry, who returned his gaze.

"Did you know the others?" Jaeger asked.

"No, but we heard," Henry said. "They warned us."

"Wolverhino don't take no prisoners," James said. "Not once, not twice, not three times, neither."

Jaeger reviewed the map and peered over his shoulder at Henry and James. Although he was not entirely sure where it might prefer to be, he thought the Wolverhino might favor upland areas, near the mountain, like a forest rhino might. Not knowing where it was, for Jaeger, was part of the fun.

"So, you both agreed to come on this hunt, despite what happened?" he asked.

"Ain't nobody come back from them other two hunts," Landon said. "Wolverhino, he don't take no hostages. But danger pays the bills, Boss."

"That it does," Jaeger said.

"Surely does," Landon said, his accent thicker than cornmeal mush.

"Of course," Sam said. "I'm hoping you nail that sucker, so we get paid and not, you know, dead."

"Gentlemen," Jaeger said. "Let me reassure you that I have no intention of being taken down by Gaiacon's pet monstrosity, and every intention of claiming their reward."

"I hear ya, Boss," Landon said. "Hear ya talking. You got that elephant gun, think Wolverhino gonna go down smooth as sin with a long gun like that?"

"I hope so," Jaeger said, as much as he understood what the man was asking of him. Landon James stroked his beard with one hand, the other hand hanging on the steering wheel.

"That ol' double barrel?" Landon asked. "Two shots? You think you can bag Wolverhino with only two damned shots?"

"I should think so," Jaeger said. "And I've also brought along a .50 revolver and my favorite hunting knife for the coup de grâce, should it come to that."

Sam scoffed. "Nerves of steel, my man. Nerves. Of. Steel."

Although there was no way of knowing for sure, Jaeger felt very confident in Beauty. She'd gotten him through a score of big game hunts, and was all that a hunter could ask for: reliable, accurate, unfussy, and precise. When he fired her, her aim was true. She was a well-worn weapon, but, in his mind, well-worn weapons were the best. They had proven themselves in battle.

"Wolverhino gonna take your two shots, Boss," Landon said. "He gonna take them two shots and come lookin' for more, gonna coup de grâce your backside with that big horn of his. Gonna split you like a log."

"Lovely image, Landon," Jaeger said.

Jaeger took a nip of bourbon from a monogrammed silver flask he kept. It had been a gift from Tilda, from their early years together. He popped the hatch overhead, wanting to get a bit of fresh air and to not have the patter of the men throw him off his game. He took scent of the air, which smelled of pine, snow, peat, and abundant earth. They were welcoming scents, familiar.

He took binoculars and again scanned around them, seeing not a trace of the fabled beast. Jaeger could hear James and Henry grousing about the cold air he was letting in by opening the hatch. Fog filled the taiga, turned the pine trees into an army of apparitions. The beast could have been anywhere, and there were no signs of tracks.

"Mr. Henry," Jaeger said. "You'll be accompanying me on foot once we've sighted the beast. Can I rely on you to remain unobtrusive?"

"You won't even know I'm there, Jaeger," Sam said. "I promise you that."

"Fabulous," Jaeger said, slipping back down, closing the overhead hatch.

"Wolverhino gonna open this ol' jeep up like a can o' beans," James muttered in a monotone to himself, gripping the steering wheel with both hands, now.

"Mr. James," Jaeger said. "It's not 'Wolverino'—it's 'Wolverhino.' Your pronunciation makes it sound like a hot cereal."

Landon blew that off with a scornful scoff.

"Could use me a warm bowl of 'Wolverino' all the same, I tellya," Landon said. All three of the men chuckled. Jaeger decided he liked Landon and Sam, and was grateful for their company.

Sam pointed at some wreckage ahead of them, about 50 yards away, taking out his video camera.

"That would be Jilton's jeep," Sam said.

"Pull up," Jaeger said, popping the hatch and bringing up his rifle, just on the off-chance that the Wolverhino might be around, although he prayed it would not be. He wanted the hunt to last. "How long ago did Jilton attempt his hunt?"

"About five weeks ago," Sam said.

"And Christoph?" Jaeger asked.

"About a dozen weeks ago," Sam said.

The wreckage was an overturned, hunter green Range Rover, torn nearly in half. Jaeger had them bring their own vehicle up to it, had them stop. He hopped out, Sam on his heels, filming.

The Range Rover looked like it had taken incoming artillery fire, so profound was the damage. And there was an overpowering musk that had Landon coughing.

For Jaeger, it was just another part of it. Every animal had their own distinctive scent. He didn't mind. Scent jogged memory like few other things.

How Jilton had been so readily caught off-guard was perhaps more concerning. He'd been a careful man, and a careful hunter. Jilton had spent the last few years as a glorified safari guide for wealthy patrons. Maybe he'd gone soft. The Wolverhino had demolished the jeep.

"Why'd they leave the jeep here?" Jaeger asked.

"Maybe they didn't want to risk sending a crew in to recover it," Sam said.

"They brought back the bodies, though," Jaeger said.

"Yeah, but that's probably easier than trying to haul back this mess," Sam said.

"Wolverhino don't like nobody messin' with his stuff," Landon said. "What a stink."

"Thiols," Jaeger said, making a mental note of the dreadful stink of it, almost as bad as a skunk. It was unforgettable.

"You'd think they would have bred that out of their creation," Sam said, gagging a bit.

But as Jaeger surveyed the damage, he thought rather it was a deliberate feature of the Wolverhino. It was impossible to ignore. The scent was unmistakably strong, and if this was a bellwether for the Wolverhino, tracking it should be relatively easy.

And, speaking of tracks, he walked around the far side of the wreckage, noting the monstrous prints of the beast, which looked about as wide as a manhole cover, tipped with claws that left deep imprints in the soil. They were magnificent tracks, and the stride of the creature was considerable. The ground likely shook when it was up to speed. Jaeger put his boot next to the track, marveled at its size, and the depth of the print on the frozen ground.

Sam filmed the wrecked Range Rover, then panned the camera around to Jaeger, who was kneeling by the great prints.

"Wolverhino gets extra traction with them ol' claws of his," Landon said, tapping a revolver he kept by his side, holstered.

Jaeger studied the approach of the thing, could see that it had come charging out of the trees, clearly surprising Jilton and his team. He wondered if the creature was nocturnal. If it were, it might present some particular challenges.

"These tracks are fresh," Jaeger said. "Not tied to the attack. It came back, surveyed the area, marked its territory."

"Damn right it marked it," James said. "Phew!"

"You can see where it struck them," Jaeger said, pointing in the direction of a stand of trees about a hundred yards distant. "It came out at them and knocked the jeep right over. Even loping about, its stride is massive. It can clear a lot of ground quickly. Jilton was entirely unprepared for that kind of speed."

Jaeger strolled around the scene, where there were still old bloodstains on the overturned jeep, scattered here and there, protected from the elements and the sun.

"Jilton was thrown clear of the jeep at the point of impact," Jaeger said, crouching by a fallen tree where he'd seen the pictures of Jilton's death. "I think he died instantly. His companions, on the other hand, not so quickly. One died when the vehicle was torn apart. The other attempted to flee that way, only to be chased down by the Wolverhino and gored about 25 yards down that way."

Landon shook his head, pointing to a dung heap down the way that would have gone up to his waist, had he been up close to it.

"Sheeit. Wolverhino's markin' his prop somethin' fierce," he said.

"I'd say it's deeper in the forest. Rhinos are remarkable for their ability to blend into the brush, despite their great size. The Wolverhino surprised Jilton."

Jaeger admitted to feeling profound exhilaration at the hunt. He felt bad for poor Jilton, the self-styled "Dragon of Borneo"—he had been completely outmatched. While he'd been something of a competitor of Jaeger's, Jilton had a sterling reputation. But the Wolverhino had bested him handily.

He thought Jilton's team had been trying to make for the taiga, perhaps around sunset, when the thing had struck them. What footage they had was garbled and badly damaged in the attack.

Jaeger was determined that this would not be his fate, looked up at the grey morning sky.

"Alright, Gentlemen, back into the jeep," Jaeger said, glancing back the way they had come. In the distance, the great wall Gaiacon had built surrounded them like a massive grey belt garlanded by a sea of swirling fog.

Sam was filming him, and was, indeed, unobtrusive, despite his endless camera work.

"We'll take the road into the forest, but we're likely to be traveling across rough country soon," Jaeger said.

"No worries," Sam replied.

"Don't forget: I'm just the driver," Landon said. "I'll wait for y'all in the Rover once you get to steppin' out."

"That's fine, Mr. James," Jaeger said, slipping back into the Land Rover. He could feel the thing out there, somewhere. The territory they had given it was lavish for a bull, far and away more territory than it required, being nearly 140 square miles.

Landon took the jeep up into the high ground, through the rough road, the trees looming around them. After seeing the wreckage of Jilton's jeep, Jaeger kept his eyes peeled for anything out of the ordinary. He would not allow the thing to flank them, if he could possibly avoid it.

"I should think that, regardless of the outcome of this hunt, Gaiacon intends to breed the Wolverhino aggressively," Jaeger said. "With this amount of territory, there'll be crashes of Wolverhinos herding here in no time."

"We saw a Wolverhino crash back yonder with Jilton's jeep," Landon said.

"No," Jaeger said. "A group of rhinos is called a 'crash,' Mr. James. If they haven't already, Gaiacon will craft some cows for our lone bull and before you know it, calves."

"Assuming you don't kill it, first," Sam said.

"Regardless of what I do," Jaeger said. "It's what they'll do. The cost of the retention wall around this reserve alone represents a significant investment on their part. There'll be more of them, just for a return on the investment."

The Land Rover bounced on the rough road awhile, and the men were in their own heads. Some ravens were flying about, wheeling around in the sky.

"That way," Jaeger said, pointing in the direction of the ravens.

Once he properly began stalking it, Jaeger intended to stay upwind of the beast and try to get close enough to shoot it. With a whole day's hunt ahead of him, he felt confident that he'd find it. Then again, if it was elusive quarry, it might take many days. He was in no hurry, was enjoying himself.

Jaeger played his own version Jilton's failed hunt in his mind: Jilton searching, not seeing, and the Wolverhino ambushing them, charging out and striking the jeep. Jilton flying through the air, screaming, only to meet his death when he struck the ground. His men died next, with the driver torn apart when the monster destroyed the jeep, and his photographer running away from the scene for his life, while the Wolverhino ran him down. What a nightmare that would have been, running, while the monster cleared around 65 feet per second, barreling down on him at that ungodly speed, eating distance in moments, goring and trampling him. Having dispatched the intruders, the Wolverhino fed on them all. The photographs of Jilton showed that clearly enough. It had feasted.

Jaeger wasn't ending up as fodder for the beast. One way or another, he would dispatch it. It was the only acceptable path he was willing to take.

In the confines of the Rover, there was a degree of comfort. Not too much, however. That was necessary—one should never be too comfortable on a hunt. Comfort dulled the senses.

Jaeger could not imagine rich tourists willing to risk their lives to this extent. They had much to lose. They would be reluctant to wager their lives on the thrill of this particular sort of hunt. Judging from the condition of Jilton's jeep, the Wolverhino was almost too good at its job. Gaiacon had done their work so well that nobody else would dare to take on their prize monster.

After several hours, they passed that stand of taiga, and found themselves in a clearing that was marked by a huge crater, one of many that had been found in Siberia, believed to be caused by methane buildups from melting permafrost.

It wasn't on the map, and only Jaeger's keen eyes had kept Landon from driving them right into it.

They parked the Land Rover and got out, gazed into the crater. The hole in the earth looked to be about 200 yards in diameter, and at least 100 yards deep, with sheer sides. There was water in the bottom, and the walls at the edge of the hole were prone to crumbling. It made Jaeger sad to see this thing. The world deserved better than to be pockmarked by global warming-created craters.

"Lord have mercy," Landon said. "It's like a hole in the heart of the world."

Sam filmed it, while Jaeger scanned the territory. He saw that they could take the Land Rover north of the crater, provided that Landon drove carefully. He pointed, indicating the route, and Landon nodded.

"How did Abercrombie die?" Landon asked.

"From the file, it says that he and his team were ambushed by the creature when they made camp," Jaeger said. "It set upon them and tore them to pieces."

"File said that thing pissed on their whole camp," Sam said. "I mean, like the whole damned camp."

"Wolverhino don't like campers," Landon said.

"It's territorial," Jaeger said. "It's to be expected."

It also favored ambush attacks, Jaeger noted. Both Jilton and Abercrombie had been ambushed. The

Wolverhino had eluded them, seemingly, only to spring at them out of nowhere. Those insights mattered to Jaeger.

When Gaiacon sent their recovery team to the scene, they'd found the men mostly eaten, with what was left sprayed with the creature's musk.

In his head, he was forming a bit of a dossier of his own, trying to get a sense of the Wolverhino's habits. It clearly had some fondness for nighttime activity, judging from its behavior. And, despite its stink and size, the Wolverhino managed a great degree of stealth.

"I think Abercrombie's camp was somewhere in the middle of that crater," Jaeger said. "Only the crater wasn't there at the time."

Jaeger had no desire to have himself be the victim of a methane explosion, was grateful that he'd quit smoking a decade ago. He found the crater disconcerting.

"Back in the jeep, Gentlemen," he said. "Let's clear the lip of this crater and get farther along."

They left the gaping crater, which looked like the unblinking, malevolent eye of a gigantic, chthonic god.

—

THE SIGHTING

They traveled three days along rough country, without so much as a sign of the Wolverhino, and Landon and Sam were getting impatient. Jaeger knew that big game hunts often ended in disappointment and failure, and accepted it as part of the game.

"You a soldier, Henry?" Landon asked, as they came to the end of the rough road, which turned into a clearing, a glade that hung in the shadow of a nameless, lopsided mountain festooned with green. Jaeger stepped out, analyzed some tracks, holding his rifle across his shoulder, scanned the sky. There were ravens again, gathered in the distance, in a glade.

"Former Marine," Sam said.

The two of them watched the hunter a moment, who had stepped out of the jeep, while Sam was readying his camera gear.

"Marine Corps?" Landon asked, adding emphasis on the latter word, stroking his beard while he said it.

"That's right," Sam said. "Why?"

"You know how to shoot?" Landon asked.

"Of course," Sam said. "But these days, I just shoot with cameras."

"That ol' Wolverhino shows up, I'm gonna shoot him, collect me the reward," Landon said. He said it like "RE-ward."

"I don't think that's part of the deal," Sam said. "You're just the driver. Jaeger's the one contracted to collect. We're contracted to help him."

"Ain't that how it always goes," Landon said. "To the victor goes the spoils, is how I see it."

Sam opened the door and addressed Jaeger, who was putting on a backpack with gear, held out a pack for Sam, who took it.

"What's up, Jaeger?"

"Tracks," Jaeger said, gesturing. "And look at that."

There was a messy pile of caribou in the glade, torn and mangled and half-eaten, covered with bickering ravens, dozens of the big, black birds fighting over the carrion. Sam took out his camera and began to record it, while Jaeger talked.

"You can see the tracks in the snow," Jaeger said. "Marvelous, feet like snowshoes. You can see where the thing attacked. A stunning charge, downhill, right at the caribou. Looks like it took down the male there, split him right in half, then attacked the herd, taking down another half-dozen before the rest fled into the forest. Then the greedy bastard gorged himself on caribou, left a midden heap or two to make it clear that this belonged to him."

"Wolverhino don't like to share," Landon said, from his view by the jeep.

"How recent?" Sam asked.

"Two or three days," Jaeger said. "I'd say this is less than three days old. I count seven dead caribou in all."

He sniffed the air, almost used to the pungent stink of the Wolverhino, and looked around them. Overhead, the sky was gunmetal grey, with low-hanging, increasingly sullen clouds.

"Wolverhino likes him some meat," Landon said. "He's eaten up all them caribou, sure as sin. Had himself a buffet."

The beast certainly had an appetite. It had eaten very well over the past dozen weeks. Jaeger thought more about the Wolverhino's diet. A lion usually ate anywhere from three to five days. A tiger, usually once a week. Rhinos needed to eat upward of 120 pounds of grass daily. Wolverines were primarily scavengers and opportunistic predators, with a more variable diet. Sloane had indicated that the Wolverhino was an omnivore, so its predation of the caribou may have been an opportunistic kill. It was impossible to know for sure, because of the novelty of the chimera.

It was possible, in the case of the Wolverhino, that the rhino's hefty herbivore appetite had somehow meshed with the wolverine's penchant for voracity. The Wolverhino was uncharted territory, and no doubt behaved in unexpected ways. Such was the way of chimeras, Jaeger thought.

That was something Jaeger had to remind himself—he was hunting a chimera, like Bellerophon in myth. Maybe that had been Jilton's folly, Abercrombie's error—they had approached the Wolverhino as something more akin to a conventional big game hunt, only bigger.

But, to Jaeger's mind, the Wolverhino was far more than its source DNA. It was a unique and deadly synthesis of beasts, and was not merely a different kind of animal. The Wolverhino was categorically unlike anything out there, and could not be counted on behaving in familiar ways.

Jaeger strode near the scene of carnage, the mountain of meat and broken bones, slashed and torn, sign of claw marks, the stench of musk almost overwhelming, mingled with the scent of blood.

Then he saw some dead wolves on the far side of the pile of caribou, their bodies split asunder and stomped flat into the frozen grass.

"Three dead wolves here," Jaeger said, pointing. "They must have tried to get at the Wolverhino's kill when it had been feeding."

"Oh, Wolverhino don't like that," Landon said. "He don't like that one bit."

Jaeger studied the wolf carcasses, felt sympathy for them. They were only doing what they'd been doing here for tens of thousands of years. Wolves sometimes killed wolverines. To the pack, the Wolverhino might have only appeared to be a massive, deformed wolverine. The wolves hadn't reckoned with running into a monster.

He walked toward the Wolverhino's dung heap and studied it, could see ground-up bone in it, along with straw. It was absurd to imagine such a creature feeding on meat that way, what contortions Gaiacon had to do to create this thing. Their gene sequencing had to have been powered by the most powerful of computers. And to what end? To create amusements for those able to afford them?

"I'm sure you'll look forward to getting some shots of the creature feeding," Jaeger said. Sam just filmed, carefully stepping this way and that.

"Which way did it go?" Sam asked.

Jaeger cleared the dung heap and followed the spoor, feeling terribly excited as he watched the sure strides of the elusive beast, heading off into the taiga, going uphill, from the look of things.

He dug out his radio, called up Landon, preferring not to shout back to him.

"Stay put, Landon," Jaeger said. "Sam and I are going on foot."

"Alright, Boss," Landon said.

He and Sam stalked into the edge of another mass of taiga, mindful of the tracks the Wolverhino had left. Jaeger was grateful that it was almost winter, wondered how the creature would fare in deep winter. Would it love the cold, or would it hate it? Would it become still more voracious, or slip into a torpor?

Glancing around him, he could see that there was a lake to the east of their position, and, in the far distance, the great wall that enclosed the Gaiacon reserve, like a manmade mountain range.

"It likely has a den somewhere," Jaeger said. "Perhaps evicting a bear."

"Now, that would be something to see," Sam said.

"I have no doubt it would prevail," Jaeger said. "The poor bear wouldn't know what hit it."

The spruce, fir, and pine trees around them were dense and plentiful, and the thick carpeting of pine needles made the ground very soft, made everything dark around them. It also made it particularly still, with only the chilly, intermittent breeze offering a sound.

Jaeger kept his rifle at the ready, leveled his eyes on the faint trail he followed, his ears pricked for anything. The stink of the beast was apparent, even now, which, mingled with the scent of pine and the smell of moss and lichens, threw off Jaeger's own seasoned sense of smell.

His radio clicked on.

"Boss," Landon said, whispering.

"Go ahead, Landon," Jaeger said.

"Wolverhino's here, Boss," Landon said.

"I know," Jaeger said. "We're stalking it."

"No, Boss," Landon said. "I mean he's right here. He's lookin' right at me."

Jaeger exchanged a glance with Sam, and the two of them turned on their heels and ran back to the edge of the glade, stopping just at the tree line. Here, they could remain under cover, screened from the poor vision of the monster.

And sure enough, at the other side of it, past the pile of caribou corpses, beside the Land Rover, several hundred yards away, was the Wolverhino.

The great beast was spectacular in the flesh, and Sam gasped, filming it, while Jaeger calculated which way the wind was blowing. They were currently downwind of the thing, which was perfect.

It strode around the Land Rover, its hulking form dwarfing the Rover, muscles rippling on its mountainous, furry frame. To see it was to behold a terror that defied reason, this sinister synergy represented in the face of the creature. Its dull button eyes were the size of silver dollars. Its broad nose and toothy maw upstaged only by its dreadful, curved horn. Its furry ears working as it tracked sound, taking sure steps along the ground. Its padded feet ended in cream-colored claws that were as long as steak knives and thick as roofing nails.

"Magnificent and horrible," Jaeger whispered.

"Unbelievable," Sam said, filming.

More colorful in person than from the demo Sloane had shared, its color was grey-brown, like black coffee and cigarette ash. The Wolverhino's hide was thick and furry. It lacked the bare, leathery skin of its rhino parentage. Rather, its fur resembled that of a wild boar's—almost bristly. The face of the thing was a true horror. It had all the capricious mindlessness of its rhino bloodline married to the malevolent, snarling fearlessness of the wolverine. Its stride was forward with a loping side-to-side, like an unnerving and restless pendulum. There was nothing ungainly about it. Its movements conveyed only raw power and abundant ferocity.

Sam recorded it, his camera quietly tracking the Wolverhino's movements. His hands were steady. Sometimes, in the presence of big game, one's nerves went. But Sam had strong nerves, and kept his composure. Jaeger appreciated this.

From his position, Jaeger would not be able to get a killing shot at this distance, so he crept toward the thing, praying the wind didn't change, trying to use the lay of the land to screen him from the Wolverhino.

"It smells me," Landon said.

"Keep quiet, Landon," Jaeger said, turning down his radio. Sam held his position by the trees, filming it nonstop since its appearance.

The Wolverhino shouldered the jeep, the Land Rover bobbing on its shocks at the force. The thing grunted, then snarled, giving the Land Rover another shove with its body. It was an aggressive move, a territorial move.

Then it raised its head and snuffed the air a bit, bared its great fangs and let out a grunt-roar that shook snow off the trees. This prompted Landon to turn on the electric engine of the Land Rover, and to attempt to back up.

"Landon, no!" Jaeger said, but Landon, in a panic, threw the Land Rover into reverse, which enraged the Wolverhino, prompting it to trot after the jeep. As expected, its trot created a percussive, piledriver thump in the ground that Jaeger and Sam could feel, even as far as they were.

Thump-thump-thump-thump.

Jaeger was still out of effective range to risk the shot. He took advantage of the monster's distraction at the hands of Landon to run after it, still using the caribou carrion as a screen, even as the ravens took to flight, the great black birds fluttering away from the caribou and taking to the trees.

The Wolverhino snarled at the Land Rover and moved into a roaring gallop, while Landon spun the jeep around and floored it, spitting dirt in the creature's eyes, which only further inflamed it, driving it to bellow at him and charge faster still.

"Wolverhino don't like me none, Boss," Landon said, skidding and fishtailing down the rough road, the Wolverhino chasing him.

To his credit, Landon managed to keep control of his vehicle, while the Wolverhino pursued. Landon floored it, and put distance between himself and the Wolverhino. It abruptly turned away from its pursuit, heading back into the cover of the trees.

"Holy shit," Sam said, still filming.

Jaeger knew it was still out of effective range, and once it got into the trees, they'd lose it. He tried to adjust his position, but there was simply no good shot for him.

"Wolverhino can't outrun a Land Rover, y'all," Landon said, with evident relief. But Jaeger's eyes were on the Wolverhino, which had slipped into the trees. For something so large, it seamlessly vanished, its unusual camouflage serving it well in the shadowy depths of the woods.

"Damn it, I've lost sight of it," Jaeger said. "Landon, pick us up.

—

THE ENCAMPMENT

JAEGER HAD, DESPITE THE CREATURE'S ESCAPE, BEEN pleased with the initial encounter. He'd gotten a good look at it, and had been able to mark its position, for purposes of tracking.

Landon had picked them up and driven them several hundred yards away from the last known location of the Wolverhino, and Jaeger had prepared himself accordingly.

"We can't very well go driving around looking for it," Jaeger said. "I'm going after it on foot."

Landon's green eyes went big at the prospect of that.

"In there? Wolverhino will tear you right up, Boss," Landon said.

"It's in there," Jaeger said. "I have to go in after it."

Sam sighed, shaking his head.

"No way am I going in there with you," Sam said. "That's you, and you alone, my friend. I'll watch from a safe distance."

"There isn't any safe distance, where that thing is concerned," Jaeger said.

Jaeger was fine with that. In many ways, he was more comfortable with that. While it was nice to have others along, it wasn't necessary. And, in the case of something like this, perhaps undesirable.

"It doesn't like the Rover," Jaeger said. "Clearly. That's something we can use to our advantage."

Landon liked the sound of that even less.

"What, you want the Rover to be bait?" Landon asked.

"Obviously," Jaeger said. "If its beady eyes are on you, they won't be on me. I only need a few moments for the perfect shot."

"Oh, that's all," Landon said.

Sam was having none of that.

"Okay, if you're saying the Rover's the bait, I'm tempted to set up cameras for it, man. I mean, that thing was huge. Like an ugly-ass truck with claws and teeth. Maybe we'll catch it taking down the Rover."

Jaeger wasn't going to debate it with them. With the way the thing moved, it could be half a mile away, already. He wanted to track it, needed to. The sighting was everything. Even as the day was waning.

"Look, you chaps sort yourselves out as you like," Jaeger said. "I'm going out after it."

"What'll we do while you're gone, Boss?" Landon asked.

"Keep in radio contact," Jaeger said. "With discretion. Now, drive me up to the edge of the woods, where the thing disappeared, and let me get out. Then you can pick me up when it's all over. We'll stay in touch by radio."

"Alright, Boss," Landon said. "But it's your funeral. Wolverhino don't like shenanigans."

"I'm taking my chances with you," Sam said, looking at Jaeger. "Or at least I'll stay at the edge of the trees. Can't say I'll go in with you, but no way am I hanging out in the Rover."

Landon scoffed.

"It's going to be nighttime soon," Landon said. "You guys going to rough it out there or what?"

"Yes," Jaeger said. "As necessary."

"It's cold," Landon said.

"We've got a few hours until dark," Jaeger said. "If I can't track it, we'll radio you and you can pick us up. Then we'll find ourselves a good spot to camp and set up."

Jaeger hopped out of the Rover as Landon stopped it near the edge of the woods. Outside, the quiet was apparent, and the scent of the Wolverhino still present. Jaeger headed off the way it had gone, having loaded Beauty.

Yes, it was cold, but it wasn't that cold, yet. And Jaeger hadn't planned on needing to camp, necessarily. He planned on tracking the Wolverhino and shooting it.

Sam came out, having set himself up with a headset camera along with his handheld.

"Wait up, Jaeger," Henry said, filming him.

"Just don't get in my way, Sam," Jaeger said. "We're going into the woods, now. Kindly keep quiet. Monsters about and all of that."

The Land Rover drove off, with Landon taking a circuitous route around the scene of the caribou slaughter, at Jaeger's direction.

"How much battery power does that Rover possess?" Jaeger asked.

"About five days," Sam said. "He's got the generator in the trunk, although when the Rover's out of juice, it'll take about a day for it to fully recharge."

"Got it," Jaeger said. He could see the Wolverhino's tracks clearly in the undergrowth in the woods. The beast seemed to just be wandering. That was okay with him. Wandering was good.

It implied that the thing was relatively relaxed, versus actively hunting. Having gorged itself on caribou only two days earlier, Jaeger hoped it would be less inclined to hunt. However, he wouldn't take any chances.

The canopy of trees overhead made it exceedingly dark on the ground, and Sam tramped close behind Jaeger, keeping quiet, otherwise.

The monster's trail took them through the dense trees, toward a rocky outcropping.

Jaeger wondered how it would work with the Wolverhino. Had they already bred herds of Wolverhino cows? Were they in some secret Gaiacon facility somewhere? Would the company have gone that far in the investment? Of course they would have. If the Game Changer initiative somehow fell through, they might be able to market their monstrosities as part of some new sort of zoo.

Jaeger wondered what kind of public outcry might occur around Gaiacon's chimeras, or whether there even would be. No, there was always an outcry over new and unusual things. And if the Wolverhino was only one example, there had to be many more.

The creature's trail led northwest, but the sun was giving up the day, and, as much as he craved the pursuit, Jaeger had no desire to hunt the Wolverhino in the dark. That kind of hubristic effort would get them killed.

"Landon," Jaeger called into his radio. "Any sign?"

"No sign, Boss," Landon said. "Where are you fellas?"

They reached some rocks in the woods, and Jaeger scaled them readily, finding a nice spot for them at the summit, where a slab of stone formed a kind of flat top. He walked around it, noting the lichen growth and searched for signs of the Wolverhino. It appeared to not have ascended to this point, and, by Jaeger's estimation, it would not be able to, despite its daggerlike claws.

Sam ascended the rocks as well, while Jaeger sniffed the air, noting the waning light.

"We should camp here," Jaeger said.

"Fine by me," Sam said. "You think that thing can't get up here?"

"With those claws it has, anything's possible, but I see no sign of scratches on the stones up here, and don't think it's that much of a climber at 9000 pounds, to be honest. I could be wrong, but I doubt it," Jaeger said. Then, to his radio, "We've found a safe camping site. We're going to camp tonight. You should go somewhere safe, yourself, Landon. But stay in radio contact."

"Where's safe around here, Boss?" Landon asked.

"Put some distance between you and the woods," Jaeger said. "At least a few miles. Make the Wolverhino work to reach you, and it'll be less likely to have a go at you. Radio in at dawn and resume your patrolling at the edge of the woods. Also, you might want to charge up the Rover during the night. I'd not like for it to run dry when you're near us. We may need to drive quickly."

"Copy that, Boss," Landon said. "Anything else?"

"That's all for now," Jaeger said. "Jaeger out."

Jaeger was pleased that Sam had brought a Quick-Tent™ among his gear. The apparatus blossomed with a push of a button, snapping into a bright red bubble that he went about securing with a slender rock hammer.

Jaeger lent a hand, securing two of the lines.

"When I was younger, I would turn my nose up at contrivances like these, but now that I'm older, I find I quite appreciate them," Jaeger said.

"Marine Corps teaches us old school camping," Sam said. "But in the field, they give us QuickTents. They have adaptive camouflage, too. Pretty sweet. Quick and easy."

He stowed his gear in half the tent, while Jaeger surveyed the interior. There was a pair of autofill cushions, as well. Nothing too fancy, but infinitely better than sleeping on cold, solid rock. Further, it astounded Jaeger that this contraption could unfurl itself so readily at the push of a button. He felt positively obsolete. Jaeger took off his pack and set it down on his side of the tent.

Then he turned back outside and climbed to the lip of the rock, while the last of the sun went away, bathing them in Siberian darkness.

The night sky overhead was stunning to behold. It was a vivid pile of diamonds as bright as one could like against the unlit sky. Jaegar had forgotten how precious lack of light pollution really was. It had been far too long since he'd been in rough country in this way.

"Gorgeous skies, Sam," Jaeger said. "Truly beautiful."

"Yeah, they are," Sam said. "I don't get these in Baltimore. It's why I took up field photography, to be honest. Places like these."

Jaeger hadn't been hunting since Tilda had died. So much of their dance had been a contrary one—as a hunter, he took life. As a conservationist, she preserved it. But they had an understanding, and a mutual respect. And, despite it all, hunters were, more often than not, avid conservationists. There was no joy in hunting in a landfill. Nature, in all her cruel beauty, had to be preserved.

"It is precious," Jaeger said. "Beyond imagining. My late wife would have enjoyed the GEAR, although she would have lobbied fearlessly to have Gaiacon turn it into a wildlife sanctuary, versus it being a proving ground for one of their bioweapons."

"Bioweapons," Sam said. "You sound cynical, Jaeger."

"I am cynical, Sam," Jaeger said. "But what's a cynic really but a wounded idealist, when you get down to it?"

Sam had managed to capture that on film, and Jaeger belatedly realized that. He chuckled to himself.

"Captured that for posterity, did you?"

"Of course," Sam said. "Had to, man."

—

THE ATTACK

The Wolverhino came for them at midnight.

Earlier in the evening, they had made an ad hoc fire atop the rock, after carefully acquiring some scrap wood around the forest floor, which itself had been an effort.

Sam had gone down to the ground while Jaeger had kept watch with Beauty. But the beast had not turned up, and they'd made the small fire in peace, and had a dinner from some mealkits both had brought. It had been a companionable evening, and they'd retired to their tent at ten o'clock.

The plan had been for them to follow that northwest trail at dawn, to see where it might lead.

The Wolverhino had other plans for them.

A light sleeper, Jaeger had been awakened by the snorting of the thing, which brought him to his feet at once. The QuickTent™ was warm, but the sound outside chilled Jaeger to his bones. He slipped on his boots and grabbed Beauty, unzipped the tent and stepped out into the chill night air.

The moon wasn't out that night, and so all around Jaeger was the darkness of the forest and that beautiful night's sky. But he could hear the snuffling of the beast in the shadows, and its monstrous, two-toned kind of moan-grunt. And, of course, the abominable stink of the thing.

"Sam," Jaeger whispered. "Wake up. It's here! Grab a flare."

Sam was up at once, and Jaeger could hear him rooting around in his pack for a flare.

Meanwhile, Jaeger crouched atop the rock, calling to the Wolverhino.

"I hear you, Thunderer," Jaeger said. "Where are you? Let's have a look at you, shall we?"

The thing clearly heard him, judging from the grunting roar it let loose. In the darkness of the forest, however, the sound echoed, and Jaeger couldn't isolate the source. The Wolverhino charged at the rock, a thundering effort, smashing into the outcroppings, causing what felt to Jaeger like a minor earthquake.

Despite crouching, Jaeger lost his balance, and saw Beauty tumble from his grasp, clattering down amid the rocks and shadows.

"Dammit!" Jaeger said, while the Wolverhino struck the rocks again, causing the great slab to shift and rocks to tumble.

Jaeger drew his sidearm, his .50 Havilland breech-loading revolver with the paracord lanyard, and quickly put the lanyard around his neck, while aiming the pistol in the dark, holding it out from him.

"Where are you, Thunderer?" Jaeger asked. Sam had finally managed to conjure up a flare, and snapped the thing to life, bathing the woods around them with a hellish red glow.

In this sort of light, the shadows took on a life of their own, and Sam held the thing aloft, trying to give Jaeger the best possible visibility.

The Wolverhino grunt-roared again, and, for a moment, Jaeger saw the bull—a hulking, monstrous shadow, its pig eyes glaring at them with unnatural rage. Although he'd wanted to use Beauty on the beast, the Havilland would do. He took aim, only to have the thing bolt as he'd pulled the trigger. The Havilland roared, but the shot went wide of the mark, only winging the Wolverhino across its back.

It had already taken off, moving with that unbelievable speed it possessed, heading northwest.

"You scared it off," Sam said.

"Unlikely," Jaeger said. His main concern was finding Beauty at the moment, hoping that she was undamaged.

But he was right about the Wolverhino. It was not yet done with them.

Rather, it had circled around their camp, coming at them from the other side, where the tent was. It grunt-roared yet again, ramming the other side of the outcropping, sending still more rocks falling. Jaeger could hear its great claws scratching at the stone, trying to find purchase.

"It's coming for us," Jaeger said, incredulous. He could not see the thing scaling the rocky outcropping, but it was certainly trying, gouging grooves in the rock, by the sound of it.

Jaeger managed to find his footing and was making his way toward the QuickTent™, which was, unfortunately, blocking his view of the Wolverhino. The thing was struggling to ascend, and then managed to take a swipe at their tent with one of its hellish forelimbs. The tent buckled and sheared before the force of the blow, and the Wolverhino let out another two-toned roar, before lurching back the way it had come and disappearing into the darkness of the woods as Sam's flare burned itself out.

"Bloody quick," Jaeger said, blinking the motes of light from his eyes, trying to recover his night vision in time. He fired a blind shot with the Havilland, the great pistol coughing loudly in the dark after the Wolverhino, but it was already gone.

Sam had managed to recover a flashlight, and shined it on the tent, whistling. Where the thing had attacked them, there was a savage slash, four claw marks, as if a band of raging Cossacks had struck the tent with sabers.

When he was confident it was gone, Jaeger holstered the Havilland and fetched his own flashlight, then went out among the rocks and hunted for Beauty. He found her wedged in a crevice, and, with some effort, managed to pry her free.

Satisfied, he climbed back up and examined Beauty by flashlight. Aside from a couple of dings, she was otherwise unharmed. She'd been through much worse in their many years together. All the same, he checked her carefully.

"Damn," Sam said. "Glad we weren't in that tent when that thing struck."

"Yes," Jaeger said. "Would have been…unpleasant. I'm more intrigued at the thing attempting to climb the rocks. A few more blows, and it might have dislodged us. Then we really would have seen something. Speaking of that, did you catch any of that with your camera?"

"You know it," Sam said. "When I'm on these sort of safaris, I wear a headcam to sleep. That way, if something happens, BAM, I got it. Shaky, but you know, I got it."

He tapped his forehead, revealing the headcam. Jaeger laughed.

"Always prepared," Jaeger said. "Well-played, Mr. Henry."

The Wolverhino behaved curiously, uniquely. It was not mindlessly hostile. Jaeger wondered what thoughts might be brewing in its thick, capricious skull. And something else surged within it. A unique animosity, as if it was angry at this world that even birthed it.

As he and Sam took stock of their encampment and kept a ready eye out for a return of the Wolverhino, Jaeger's mind wandered around those notions. He'd already outlasted Jilton and Abercrombie both. But Jaeger had faced the Wolverhino twice, now, and had emerged intact and unscathed. So, there was that, at least.

Jaeger sometimes played back encounters in his head, to take a proper reckoning of what had occurred, at least as much as he remembered it. The Wolverhino had gone at them, but it was also more circumspect than he'd expected.

He wondered how the thing was brought up, what this vat-grown abomination's life had been before being deployed to the GEAR. Ms. Ketteridge had not been very forthcoming about Gaiacon's genetic engineering program. He told himself the Wolverhino was ultimately no different from any other livestock—bred for the slaughter.

In fact, when he was a kid, during the waning days of Big Agriculture, after most people had given up on a meat-based diet, he'd seen the gradual winnowing of livestock into near-oblivion. The massive industrial ranches of cattle and pig farms, the endless cages of chickens—they had themselves faded into history, with only locally-sourced, boutique farmers still tending small gatherings of livestock in free range areas.

Gaiacon could be seen, as absurd as it appeared with the money the company had, as just another boutique agricultural enterprise. The only difference was that, instead of growing animals to be turned into meat, they were growing them to be hunted.

All the same, he wondered what the life of the Wolverhino had been. A native-born rhino could live anywhere from 30 to 50 years. A wolverine had a much shorter lifespan, somewhere between five to a dozen years. What, then, was the lifespan of the Wolverhino? Averaging in his brain, he guessed anywhere from 16 to 30 years.

The creature out there was a full-grown bull, which likely meant that Gaiacon had originally begun their program more than a decade ago. Which, itself, was somewhat fascinating to Jaeger.

Someone at Gaiacon had gotten the bright idea likely thirty years ago, implemented it perhaps twenty years ago, and had gotten a viable product in the Wolverhino a decade ago. That kind of enterprising strategic vision was alien to Jaeger. The scope and scale of it was breathtaking.

And, more than not, it left him a little cold. Thirty years ago, he'd been on an African safari with Tilda. They'd been in their 30s. The waning of the old world had been in full swing back then.

A grunt-roar from the Wolverhino shook Jaeger out of his reverie. He and Sam exchanged glances in the dark.

"He's out there," Sam said.

"Oh, yes," Jaeger said. "I don't think we'll be getting much more sleep tonight."

And he was nearly right.

—

THE CALL

Despite their situation, the two men took turns napping on the rock. That had been the gentlemen's agreement between them. This was an encampment that required being on watch. Which meant that Jaeger let Sam sleep for four hours while he took first shift, and he took the following four. They'd discussed it, and while Jaeger wanted to be up at dawn, he decided it was better for them to at least attempt more rest, and the four-hour bloc was agreed upon.

Grunt-roars aside, the Wolverhino had ranged away from them. Always northwest, Jaeger noted. Its den had to be somewhere over that way.

He had insisted on taking the first watch, just in case the Wolverhino doubled back to have another go at them, but the thing had not returned.

While Sam slept, Jaeger was alone with his thoughts. If he had not taken up Gaiacon's challenge, the lugubrious Lester Kishwalla would absolutely have taken up the quest. The man approached big game hunting with the burlesque brutality of a half-mad gladiator. It was simply unacceptable for a man like Kishwalla to have claimed the prize.

With their monstrous menagerie, Gaiacon had, in their curious and decades-spanning vision, breathed new life into what was a dying sport. Game Changers, indeed.

His radio clicked to life, and he was surprised to hear Ms. Ketteridge calling in.

"Still among the living, Mr. Jaeger?" Sloane asked.

"Yes, Ms. Ketteridge," Jaeger replied.

"Our satellites indicated some trouble earlier," Sloane said.

"Nothing we couldn't handle," Jaeger said. He glanced skyward, wondered what their spy satellites were seeing.

"That's good to know," Sloane said. "We had some concerns that maybe you were dead."

"Not just yet," Jaeger said. "Tell me, Ms. Ketteridge, how old is this bull I'm hunting?"

A pause before replying.

"Eight years," Sloane said.

"So, fully grown at eight years," Jaeger said.

"In his prime," Sloane said.

"Gaiacon must have, what, game preserves for these chimeras, then?"

"We do, naturally," Sloane said. "Breeding grounds."

Naturally, indeed.

"You've created breeding stock," Jaeger said. "A significant investment."

"Of course," Sloane said. "Much of the Game Changer program is front-loaded, in terms of cost. Once we've created a viable specimen, we decant them and create breeding pairs. After that, things take care of themselves, and there's only a matter of maintenance and upkeep. Nominal, contrasted with Gaiacon's other areas of activity."

Jaeger imagined this strange Gaiacon preserve, with Wolverhinos ranging upon it, as well as the other, as-yet-confidential proprietary creations Gaiacon was no doubt churning out.

"It still seems a substantial undertaking on the part of Gaiacon, with very uncertain outcomes," Jaeger said.

"We're confident we can develop a luxury market for our Game Changers," Sloane said. "You'd be surprised what people will do for the thrill of something truly new. With our massive genomic archive and advanced breeding program, we've got the capacity to deliver new creatures to market on a level that would leave you breathless, Mr. Jaeger."

Her cool, corporate confidence was chilling across the radio, in the dark of the predawn.

"There are always clients willing to pay," Sloane said. "You should be thankful you're getting to product test with us. It's a measure of our respect for your skills, Mr. Jaeger."

Not that much respect, he thought.

"Why didn't you pick Kishwalla over me?" Jaeger asked.

"As you yourself said, he lacks a certain finesse," Sloane said. "You're a more authentic hunter. You're more, how can I put this? Old-school in your approach. We wanted to set that standard with you, before we go to market properly."

Old-school, indeed. He doubted most of the clients who'd be hunting wolverhino would be particularly old-school. Most of them would crave some kind of canned hunt, an altogether profane manner of hunting.

"I am old-school, I suppose," Jaeger said. "Or maybe just old."

"Either way, Gaiacon sees real value in your approach," Sloane said. "Well, we're glad you're alive, and want to leave you to it, Mr. Jaeger. We'll be watching. Take care of yourself."

"You, too," Jaeger said, absurdly. He figured Ms. Ketteridge was lounging comfortably in her office, in a far more companionable time zone.

Tilda would have found the Gaiacon breeding preserves—wherever they were—offensive. She would have found the entire Game Changers program wanting. He could almost hear her reproach, in her clipped, crisply New England cadence.

"Making monsters, indeed," Tilda would have said. "Felix, it's simply dreadful. You can do better, my dear."

Her ghost left him beneath the stars, alone upon the rock, standing guard, Beauty on his shoulder, while a gentle snow fell. There was no wind, so the snowflakes drifted down beautifully, like a flock of fallen angels.

—

THE PACK

Sam woke Jaeger at the intended time, while Landon barked to them on the radio, the static crackle getting Jaeger up at once. Somewhere in the forest, a wolf howled. It was answered by another.

"Boss, Wolverhino's out here," Landon said. "He's snuffling around, hunting me. I got the Rover rolling. I charged the Rover up last night, like you said. But Wolverhino's on my six."

"Keep ahead of it," Jaeger said. In fact, he was not pleased that the Wolverhino had become fixated on the Rover. It was disappointing.

Sam pushed the button on the QuickTent™, and the mangled thing attempted to fold itself back together, but the damage the Wolverhino had done to it was too significant to mend, so the tent looked like its own kind of monstrosity, with a couple of its spindly limbs projecting outward around the frayed rags.

"Leave it," Jaeger said. "We need to get off this rock and back out there."

"Alright," Sam said, and they got their packs back on and carefully came down off the snow-dusted and slippery rock, finding solace on the softness of the forest floor. The scent of pine was pleasantly thick, here, and within the woods, there was some shelter from the chilly Siberian wind.

"Wolverhino's off my six again, Boss," Landon said. "He done tramped back into the woods about three clicks from your current location."

"Got it, Landon," Jaeger said. Excited at the prospect of going to ground with the Wolverhino again, Jaeger broke Beauty open and needlessly checked to see if she was loaded. Of course she was.

"Let's go, Sam," Jaeger said. "Just under two miles east of us. It's in the woods again."

Sam had his cameras ready, both headset and hand-held, and the two men hiked east, Jaeger's senses keenly attuned for any sign of the Wolverhino. Several more wolves howled, their voices echoing forlornly in the forest, putting the men on edge.

The Wolverhino definitely preferred the woods, Jaeger thought, over the open range. He wasn't sure why, but the creature was definitely more at home in the woods, which was curious to him, given its great size. He chalked it up to the Wolverhino's contradictory nature—aggressive yet unpredictable, savage yet furtive.

Jaeger and Sam made their way to the edge of the woods, and could see Landon's Rover some distance away, tooling around. They hiked along, Jaeger tracking in the fresh-fallen snow, grateful that it had fallen at all, as it gave him better prospects of finding the Wolverhino.

In fact, as they reached the point where the Wolverhino had vanished into the woods, Jaeger could see that the beast had left a pretty clear trail, whether by bumping into trees and dislodging what snow they had, or by tufts of fur here and there on tree trunks.

Some of the trees actually bore some scratch marks on them, as well as the telltale musk.

"Marking its territory, as ever," Jaeger said, pointing it out to Sam, who filmed. "Territorial bastard, to be sure."

"Aren't we all?" Sam said.

Jaeger radioed Landon to stay put while he and Sam went back into the woods. The creature's tracks were easy to follow in the woods. That would be pleasing to prospective hunters. Despite its ability to vanish in the trees, it left a clear trail.

Its grunt-roar sounded in the distance, echoing in the trees, putting Jaeger and Sam back on alert.

They paused, at the ready, listening for any sign of the thing. But there was nothing. They waited for a long minute, before Jaeger resumed.

After hiking for an hour, they came upon a stream that fed into a creek, which was largely frozen at this point. The Wolverhino's tracks paralleled the stream and paused at the creek, where the creature had clearly had itself a drink before going back off into the woods.

They followed the thing's tracks, which led them back to their encampment. The Wolverhino had returned to their campsite, and had attacked the Quick-Tent™ once more, having torn the thing to shreds. The rocks around their former campsite were badly scratched, with grooves like stony furrows hewn in the lichenous rock. Somewhere in the forest, wolves howled in greater number, answered by the grunt-roar of the Wolverhino.

"It came back," Sam said. "It was looking for us."

"So it appears," Jaeger said. He was intently studying the tracks, since their lives depended on Jaeger knowing just where the chimera was. There were several sets of tracks leading away from the camp, and he strained his eyes to make out which was the most current set of tracks. He could see wolf tracks paralleling the Wolverhino.

The most recent appeared to be heading south. He directed Sam to follow him that way. Every sound they made, whether the crunching of their boots in the snow, to the breeze, to the creak of trees, to the howls of the wolves, put Jaeger on edge. The scent of the Wolverhino was all around them, and growing stronger.

"You smell that?" Sam asked. He'd put a red bandana over his mouth.

"Of course," Jaeger said.

In the distance, Jaeger thought he saw movement. He held up a hand to stop Sam, and brought up Beauty, taking aim. Then they heard the howls up close, far closer than before.

Not just one or two, but a whole chorus of them. Wolves. A dozen of them, maybe more. And then, the seething grunt-roar of the Wolverhino. Something was happening up ahead.

Jaeger tramped his way toward another clearing in the forest, where a great battle was taking place. There was a great pack of wolves—mostly grey-white, and the Wolverhino, fighting each other.

The wolves snarled at the Wolverhino, which circled about, slashing at them with its already blood-soaked horn. Jaeger took stock of the situation. Two wolves were dead, while a baker's dozen were circling the Wolverhino, fangs bared.

In that clearing, the great beast shambled about, while the wolves harried it, avoiding the great horn and clawed forelimbs, while trying to nip at its back legs and tail. The harassment was absolute. The wolves gave ground without retreating, while the Wolverhino grunt-snorted at them, keeping its deadly head aimed at them in a whirling sort of dance of death.

Jaeger could see where his shot with the Havilland had grazed the Wolverhino—a nearly perpendicular mark in its thick fur.

The wolves were continuing to circle the Wolverhino, while Sam filmed, captivated.

Jaeger wondered again how the wolves would even view something like this creature. Was it seen as prey? Or perhaps as an intruder and rival?

Another wolf nipped at the tail of the Wolverhino, causing it to whip around, only to draw attacks from the other side.

Could a pack this size bring down the monster? The wolves themselves were a healthy-looking pack. Anything was possible.

Snort-snarling, the Wolverhino charged down a trio of wolves who had been trying to get at its belly, and the great beast crashed into them, flinging yelping wolves left and right of it with devastating cuts of its great horn. The wolves landed tens of feet away, their bodies torn almost in half. The power of it was incredible, and the bloody spectacle, undeniable.

"Are you going to take your shot, Jaeger?" Sam asked.

"Gods, no," Jaeger said. "This is their fight. I'm not going to intrude."

Seeing three more of their own killed by the Wolverhino only seemed to inflame the wolves, who continued their confrontation with the monster. Around and around they spun like dervishes, the Wolverhino's horn bloody down the length of it, rivulets of wolf blood dripping down its snout, splashing on the well-packed.

"Surprised the GEAR has wolves in here," Sam said.

"They likely enclosed a native habitat," Jaeger said. "Threw some money the Russians' way and built their wall around it."

By Jaeger's estimate, the wolves were acquitting themselves reasonably well against the Wolverhino, if only because they still had the numbers. As powerful as the Wolverhino was, it was only one great creature, against nine or ten big wolves. Numbers mattered in Nature.

Ignored by the wolves and the Wolverhino, the men observed the battle from what they considered a safe distance of a hundred yards.

It would have been the easiest thing in the world for Jaeger to bring Beauty up and put a killing shot into the Wolverhino. But it would not have been sporting. Above and beyond the wolves stealing his kill, there was that element of fair play that stayed Jaeger's hand. Whether living or dying, the Wolverhino had been dealt this particular hand, and Jaeger would let the thing see it through.

So, he took advantage of its distraction to study how it fought. It definitely pinwheeled about with its horn, reluctant to engage with its terrifying forelimbs, likely for fear of exposing its vulnerable belly to the more numerous wolves.

Further, despite the gnashing teeth of the wolves, precious little of the Wolverhino's own blood had been spilled. There appeared to be some superficial wounds on its hind legs, and some bites on its tail, but it was otherwise whole and mostly unharmed.

By his count, Jaeger saw perhaps five wolves dead in the snow. "Perhaps" only because the amount of damage the Wolverhino inflicted on its victims was considerable, leaving them in poor condition that made identification uncertain.

Another pair of wolves attacked, and the Wolverhino charged into them, trampling them. Their yelp-whimpers sounded as loudly as the pistol-crack sound of their bones crunching beneath the bulk of the monster. Even where Sam and Jaeger stood, the ground all but shook from the forceful mass of the thing.

The wolf pack was now reduced to seven members, and the wolves appeared to be lessening their attack, moving at wider distances, now, out of the reach of the thing's horn, while still circling and snarling. The Wolverhino huffed and puffed, great gouts of steam passing from its broad mouth, with wisps of steam rising from its thick coat.

"I think the wolves have had enough," Jaeger said, watching the pack put a wary distance between them and the chimera. The surviving wolves let out a cacophonous howl, before finally retreating into the forest.

The Wolverhino paused, then grunt-roared in answer to their howls, began nosing around the ruined wolf corpses, given them tosses as it hooked them with its horn. Again and again it threw them about, the wolf bodies spinning bloodily about, landing with thumps in the snow.

Jaeger dearly wanted to take the shot, but still stayed his hand. He didn't want to finish off what the wolves had started. The thing deserved better than that. Sam even glanced at him.

"Jaeger, now are you going to take the damned shot?" Sam asked.

"No," Jaeger said. "Not just yet. The old boy just survived a battle. He deserves to catch his breath before I take it from him."

"Sentimental as fuck," Sam said.

"Maybe," Jaeger said. He raised Beauty and got the Wolverhino in his sights. It was there for the taking. It had no idea they were there. The easiest shot in the world, under the circumstances. "Pow."

He brought Beauty down, and Sam laughed to himself.

"You're crazy, Jaeger," Sam said. "You take the shot when you get it, man."

"Is that how they do things in Baltimore, Sam?" Jaeger asked.

"Damn right," Sam said. "In Baltimore, you don't get a second shot, more often than not."

The Wolverhino played around with the wolf corpses a few minutes more, then trotted off into the woods, away from them. In the distance, unseen, now, the wolves howled. They would remember and resent it. The Wolverhino had made an enemy this day.

And, as Jaeger watched it go, perhaps it had made a friend, as well.

—

THE HIKE

When they got back to the Rover, Landon couldn't believe what Sam told him.

"You had the shot and you didn't take it, Boss?" Landon asked. "Wolverhino don't give out second chances. That sumbitch was dogging me every chance it got."

"Wolverhino don't like the Land Rover," Jaeger said. As much as he'd enjoyed the tramping in the forest, he was grateful to take a rest in the cozy confines of the vehicle.

He and Sam drank some coffee that Landon had managed to brew inside the Rover, an amenity that was available in the electric jeep.

"What now, Boss?" Landon asked.

Jaeger drank his coffee before replying.

"He was heading northwest," Jaeger said. "So, we'll drive up that way, try to get ahead of him. Not sure where he's heading, but I'm not eager to trek through wolf-infested Siberian forest to find out."

"Hazard pay, man," Landon said, driving on ahead with his characteristic bravado. He was a good driver, with a steady hand. For all of his boundless chatter, Jaeger appreciated that he was a good driver. Bad drivers got vehicles stuck, and could turn a safari into a disaster with relative ease.

Jaeger watched the countryside speed past them, which, from here, was boundless taiga, deciduous forest, and grassy clearing.

"Here there be taiga," Jaeger said, toasting it with his cup of coffee.

"I don't think there are Siberian tigers in the GEAR anymore, Boss," Landon said. "Wolverhino would kill them real quick."

"I don't know," Sam said. "Those wolves did a pretty good job against it."

"Almost," Jaeger said. "Wolves are always dangerous in those kinds of numbers. I think he acquitted himself rather well, all things considered."

He imagined the Wolverhino finding a cave somewhere out there, resting within it, dreaming whatever the Wolverhino might dream about. What, indeed, might it have thought about? Would it have appreciated the danger it evaded with that wolf pack? Or was it even capable of comprehending its good fortune and survival?

"I would have taken that shot, man," Sam said. "Although the footage I captured was top-shelf. First-rate stuff."

Sam showed them the raw footage, and Jaeger admitted that it was definitely great wildlife photography.

Landon drove them to the edge of a broad area of taiga, bringing the Rover to a halt. There was a trail that wound up from there along the rolling countryside, but the way was partially obscured by snow.

He consulted the Rover's computer map.

"Rover says there's a way over that frozen stream, but I sure can't see it, Boss," he said. "Best be careful, take this slow."

"I understand," Jaeger said. "Maybe Sam and I can get out and stretch our legs a bit more."

Landon nodded, snorting. "It's your funeral, Boss."

Jaeger finished his coffee, put it in its cup holder, glanced back at Sam, who was nursing his while reviewing footage.

"What do you say, Sam? Ready for another go?" Jaeger asked.

"Sure thing, Jaeger," Sam said, swapping out the datachip from his handheld. "I'm ready to go."

Jaeger wasn't going to admit that the poor night's sleep and hiking about had taken its toll on him, so out he went, back into the cold, while Sam geared up and followed, and Landon nursed the Rover over the snowy streambed, careful not to get stuck.

"I'm grateful for the cold, to be honest," Jaeger said. "It makes the taiga more passable when it's frozen over. If this had been summer, we'd be up to our waists in it."

"That's no good," Sam said.

Jaeger was checking the ground, as ever, and around them, for sign of the Wolverhino. The tracks he found were older, and headed northeast.

"Somewhere in there," Jaeger said, pointing. "It's got a lair in there."

"Great," Sam said. "Probably a cave full of bones."

"If we're lucky," Jaeger said.

He hiked that way, while Landon turned the Rover around, having abandoned the streambed when he saw where they were going.

"I'm gonna swing the Rover around, Boss," Landon said.

Jaeger acknowledged that and trekked deeper into the taiga, tracking the Wolverhino anew.

"It appears to stalk the perimeter of the GEAR," Jaeger said. "With some exploratory forays across the grasses. I'd love if it came at us from the grass."

"Uh, yeah," Sam said.

Jaeger saw some old, cracked caribou bones in the snow. By the look of them, the Wolverhino had crunched them down some time ago.

"Why'd you come out of retirement for this, anyway, man?" Sam asked. "I don't think you're what I'd call hurting for money."

"No," Jaeger said. "You're right about that."

He wasn't as well off as perhaps people thought, but he was better off than most. Enough so that the Gaiacon pricetag for this hunt had made it worth his time. He longed for a time when he couldn't be bought. Tilda had helped him in that regard. She could never be bought, not at any price.

Her memory lingered as he crunched his way through the frozen taiga. It had been a few hours since the fight with the wolves, but, as they went deeper into the woodland, it was clear that the Wolverhino was still restless, judging from its tracks, which crisscrossed in the woods, many of the tracks relatively recent.

Perhaps it was still hunting any outlier wolves. Or maybe it was looking for prey. As ever, the beast's behavior was difficult to comprehend, because of its novelty as an organism. There were no clear instincts or patterns Jaeger would discern for sure.

The restlessness of the Wolverhino was a curious behavior. It was not a passive beast, but, rather, was active on a level that was unusual for something so large. Jaeger didn't have any way of accounting for that.

He could relate, in some fashion. Although mostly retired, he was restless, too. In her stately and gracious way, Tilda had brought a measure of peace to him. The kind of peace he usually only felt on the hunt.

People didn't understand it. They saw only the end result, the sacrifice at the end of the hunt. They failed to see the journey, itself. For the hunter, the hunt itself was the most sacred of things, whether or not it was successful. The purity of it was unknown to those who didn't undertake it. The hunt itself was everything.

Felix felt something else, however, as he worked his way through the taiga, Sam close by, filming, always filming.

In this special hunt, this unique hunt, Jaeger was condemning the Wolverhino, and all of its kin to its own kind of hell. Bred only for death, these chimeras would be born for this fate, and this fate only.

It was a peculiar epiphany. This Wolverhino was the first of its kind. The creature would never live a natural life, or even a life of any sort of what Jaeger could only think of as joy. Gaiacon would, based on the outcome of this hunt, ready herds of the things for shipment, would place them on proprietary preserves, and market their Game Changers for clients. The Wolverhino would never know proper peace. It was a gladiator, created solely for this sort of arena.

As such, it wasn't like the big game of old. In those cases, man ventured out into the natural world and measured himself against the species that predated man, himself. But the Wolverhino was man's own creation. It was, to Jaeger's mind, an abusive relationship—as abusive as God's own fictive relationship to Man was. Maybe even more abusive, in fact.

In his own desire to return to the hunt, he'd be party to the damnation of this monster. Tilda would have dissuaded him from undertaking this hunt at all.

"Isn't there enough death in the world already, Love?" she would have said.

Jaeger had no answer for her ghost, but turned his eyes toward the tracks they followed. There were hints of blood on the ground, from where the wolves had attacked it. Not much, but enough for him to see.

"Sam," Jaeger said. "This way."

He followed the tracks and the flecks of blood, which were not many. What damage the wolves had done was nominal, despite the carnage they had witnessed.

Overhead, the conifers clutched at the sky and strangled the light from it, bathing the two men in evergreen darkness.

In these confines, Jaeger felt more vulnerable than ever. The scent of the Wolverhino was stronger, here, clashing with the ever-piquant pine.

He brought up Beauty, had her at the ready, although there was neither sight nor sound of the beast. But it was close, he was certain.

Within this area, he'd probably only have one chance for a shot at the thing before it got to them. He'd give it both barrels, and pray that they found their mark. Beauty had never failed him before. She would not fail him, now.

The radio crackled, and it was Landon.

"It's over here, Boss," Landon said. "Edge of the woods. About a click from you, due east. I think it's gunning for me. Wolverhino sure don't like the Rover."

"Alright, Landon," Jaeger said. "We're on our way."

Jaeger was conflicted, because, of course, the creature's bloodied tracks led in another direction, but the thing clearly doubled back, heading back for the frosty grassland.

"Sam, we're going to be in a near thing with the beast soon enough," Jaeger said. "I want you to be careful. Should I miss, or only wound it, we may not have a second chance."

"I understand, Jaeger," Sam said. "I'll be careful."

"Good," Jaeger said. He held his breath a moment, then changed direction, toward certain death—whether it was his own or the Wolverhino's, he did not yet know.

—

THE ROVER

As they neared the edge of the taiga, Jaeger could only see the Rover, tooling around. Frustrating as ever, the great Wolverhino was nowhere to be seen, and its tracks had crisscrossed within the woods, making tracking difficult—all he could determine was that it was here, but not precisely where.

The scent of it was dizzyingly strong, as well. It was nearby, but in the dark of the taiga, it remained elusive. Jaeger despaired finding it when the beast charged out of the woods not two hundred yards from where he and Sam were to bear down on the Land Rover, letting out its always unusual call. Landon turned the wheel of the Rover to try to move away from the beast.

What a specimen it was, its great horn still blood-soaked from the wolves, galloping toward the Rover, while Landon fought to evade it.

But the Wolverhino managed to slam into the vehicle, sending the Land Rover sliding sideways into some larches, dumping a light dusting of snow onto it and the vehicle.

Jaeger was huffing and puffing as he pursued it, while Sam had emerged from his flanking position to film on the go. Landon was calling into the radio.

"Wolverhino's coming for me, Boss!" Landon said.

The Wolverhino actually reared up and brought its great forelimbs against the back of the Land Rover, tearing the rear door off the thing with a swipe of its terrible claws, the shredded door landing like an afterthought tens of feet past the creature's shoulder, while it pried open the jeep and got at their supplies, which had been intended to last them for two weeks.

Landon drew his sidearm and fired a shot at the Wolverhino. It snarled at him, falling back and then ramming the Land Rover again, jarring the vehicle. It bounded around to the front of the vehicle, actually climbing atop it, its great bulk crushing the hood and breaking the windshield.

"Good god, Landon," Jaeger said, running hard for it, his lungs burning. "Be careful!"

Jaeger and Sam were still over a hundred yards away from the beast, Jaeger breathing harder than ever in the cold air, while the Wolverhino jumped and shoved at the Land Rover, its hoof-claws smashing the windshield as it reached in for Landon, who was pinned by the half-crushed cab and the fir tree trunk that kept the driver side door from opening.

The Wolverhino grunt-roared at him, while Landon undid his seatbelt and backslid himself across to the passenger side of the Land Rover, kicking the passenger's side door open and running out. It was the worst thing he could have done.

While it had been momentarily occupied with spraying its horrendous musk on the Land Rover, the Wolverhino could see Landon running, and it went right after him, crushing and trampling the Land

Rover as it reached the ground, thundering after Landon West like a runaway freight train.

As before, the ground rumbled beneath the thing's great feet, a galloping thump like the pounding of tribal drums—a relentless sound that heralded death and dismemberment with each impending beat. Landon was running out of time, the Wolverhino right on him, breath coming from its great nostrils in steaming jets. The thing's face was malevolence incarnate, and that great bloodied horn hung over Landon like the Angel of Death.

Jaeger dropped to one knee to steady himself with his Winchester .458, trying to slow down his breathing enough to be able to get the shot, while Landon ran into the forest across the way, spoiling his shot, as the Wolverhino changed course, kicking up chunks of dirt as it charged after the fleeing driver.

"No, Landon," Jaeger yelled. Had he run right for Jaeger, he'd have gotten the clean shot. Now, however, the thing was back in the canopy of taiga, while Landon was running for his life, screaming between the trees, the Wolverhino grunt-growling close behind him.

"Sam," Jaeger said, gesturing to the cameraman, wanting him to follow him across the trail.

Landon was shrieking into his radio.

"Wolverhino's after me, Boss!" he said. The driver would be overtaken in seconds.

"Make your way back to the trail," Jaeger said. "I need a clear bloody shot, Man."

It was, as ever, uncanny how readily the thing could vanish into the woods, despite its amazing bulk. In the dark of the taiga, there was no way Jaeger would risk a shot. He needed the thing to come back into the glade where, even robed in clouds, the sun was. Landon's pistol fired again, again, and again.

"Landon, come in," Jaeger said into the radio. "Landon, where are you?"

Jaeger then heard a great scream pierce the taiga, and then, nothing at all.

—

THE RECKONING

After waiting for a reappearance of the Wolverhino for nearly an hour, they ventured forth and found Landon wedged upside-down in a cluster of fallen fir trees, his body bent and broken, torn to ribbons and covered in musk. His radio was nearby, on the ground, crushed beneath a colossal footprint. His blood-soaked pistol, a 9mm automatic, was similarly mashed into the ground, spent casings scattered around it. The Wolverhino's tracks went back uphill, bearing east, vanishing once more into the vastness of the taiga.

Sam filmed the scene, while Jaeger offered a mournful elegy for the man, although inwardly he was angry at him for panicking. And angrier still at himself for his perfectionism—he could have squeezed off a sloppy broadside shot at the Wolverhino. Had he done so, perhaps the thing would have been killed, instead of Landon. Or, at the very least, Jaeger would have gotten the thing's attention, and it would have turned and run them down.

The mistake was his, not Landon's. He should have taken the shot. But it would have been a hasty shot—a reckless and inelegant kill.

"Landon James, our driver," Jaeger said. "And we, witnesses and survivors."

He radioed the Gaiacon rangers, reported what had happened, and where Landon was.

"It didn't eat him," Sam said. "Why didn't it eat him?"

"I don't know," Jaeger said. "Maybe it's saving him for later, or was simply angry and not hungry at all."

He did not want to attempt to track the beast in waning light in the conifer forest, so he had them circle back and make their way to the Land Rover, which looked like it had been worked over by an four-ton monster. What it had not demolished, it had sprayed with its ungodly musk.

Jaeger winced as he took in the scent. "Charming creature, to be sure. I really do want to personally thank Ms. Ketteridge for her employer's inclusion of those horrid scent glands in the manufacture of their monster."

He looked around, mindful of a few things: first, their Land Rover was destroyed, and the Wolverhino had befouled whatever they could salvage from it. Two, it would be nightfall, soon. Three, what had been a generally manageable drive would make for an exhausting, week-long hike. Four, it would get rather cold, rather soon. Five, Jaeger had no intention of conceding the day to this creature; there was simply too much at stake for him, both personally and professionally.

He pointed back the way they had come. "Sam, that way leads to what passes for civilization out here. You can radio Ivanova and they'll come get you out."

Sam looked down the way they had come, while Jaeger pointed uphill, toward the highlands that had loomed throughout the GEAR.

"That way lies the quarry," Jaeger said. "You may do as you like, Sam, but I intend to bring it down. Between us, we have gear to allow us to weather a day or two out here without need of resupply or rescue. I assure you that I plan to make the most of it."

Sam looked longingly down the road, then gazed squarely at Jaeger. "I'm with you, Jaeger."

"I appreciate it," Jaeger said, eyeing the terrain around them. "I fear more fog may be rolling in this evening. I won't be very happy about that. Let's go back to the glade."

The two of them hiked back to the glade, mindful of the ravens feasting on the caribou once more, and distant howls of wolves in the developing, enveloping dark. Besides those sounds nearby, it was silent where they were, except for a soft breeze that blew intermittently.

Jaeger pondered their next steps. Given what had happened, he had no intention of camping anywhere accessible to the Wolverhino, without precisely knowing what was not accessible to the beast, beyond that rocky pile they'd camped at what felt like a lifetime ago, which was ultimately too far away for them to navigate at the moment.

"Why didn't you shoot at it when it was charging Landon?" Sam asked.

"Are we on-camera?" Jaeger asked.

Sam shook his head. Jaeger didn't know whether or not to believe him, and decided he didn't care.

"It wasn't a clean shot," Jaeger said. "I wanted a clean shot, for a good kill."

Sam just looked at him a moment. Of course, he judged him for it. That was the only human reaction possible, under the circumstances. Jaeger replayed the moment in his head, and cursed himself for his hesitation. He should have taken the shot. It would have been an ugly, hasty shot, but Landon may have been alive, had he taken it.

"Anybody can go out and make a mess of things," Jaeger said. "I'm not like that, Sam."

"But Landon died," Sam said. "I think maybe you could have saved him. I tell you this, Jaeger: if that thing's chasing me down, you better shoot the living hell out of it. Clean or not, I want that thing dead, not me hanging upside down in some damned trees."

Jaeger nodded, drew a swig from his flask and handed it over to Sam, who partook of it as well, although his eyes were full of judgment and reproach. Jaeger was reminded of one of his hunts, twenty years ago.

"You know, I once saw a man stomped to death by a hard-bossed Cape buffalo bull. A client I was chaperoning on his own big game hunt. You have to wait until they get very close—50 yards or so, if you want to do it right. It sounds like a lot of distance, but when you see that big bull in your sights, it's damned close, and it can give you nerves. He was the client; I was just there to help him get his trophy. But he'd botched it, only wounded the beast, enraged it, and it just ran him down. He had insisted on taking the shot, and I gave it to him, rightly or wrongly. I wanted him to have his moment. And he had it, alright. After my client had gone down in a thunder of hooves, I shot that bull dead at 15 yards. His family didn't want the trophy, so I took it. 52-inch horns. Felt a sense of obligation to a dead man."

"This isn't like that, Jaeger," Sam said. "You didn't lose your nerve."

"No, I didn't," Jaeger said. "But I suppose I got greedy. And poor Landon paid for it."

"Damn right, he did," Sam said. "You should have taken the shot."

He was right, of course. Jaeger told himself he hardly knew Landon, that the man's fate was his own doing. Further, as it was ultimately his hunting expedition, the responsibility fell to him.

"Did he have family?" Jaeger asked.

"Don't we all have family somewhere?" Sam said.

"Fair enough," Jaeger said. "I don't. I've outlived everyone I ever cared about. Every last one."

"Not me," Sam said. "I've got a wife and three kids back in Baltimore."

Jaeger and Tilda had not had children. Her concern for the world's conservation precluded the possibility of parenthood for them. She had not wanted to have children, and he'd loved her enough to go along with it, although, privately, it pained him. Ultimately, he admitted, especially when he was younger, he was grateful not to have children to worry about when he was on safari. Now that he was old, however, and with Tilda gone, his world was an emptier place.

"You're very fortunate," Jaeger said. "What are they, boys? Girls?"

"Three boys," Sam said. Jaeger smiled.

"That'll keep you busy," Jaeger said.

"Oh, it does," Sam said.

Somewhere in the woods, the Wolverhino called out, its grunt-roar as distinctive as ever. It didn't sound too close, and Jaeger was somewhat grateful for that. He didn't want to have to target it at night.

"Tomorrow, I'll bag the beast," Jaeger said, watching the last rays of the sunset vanish in the sky overhead. There were clusters of clouds to catch the wayward rays, and Jaeger thought he could see shapes in them. One cloud even halfway resembled the Wolverhino to his eyes. He pointed, commenting on it. Sam laughed, filmed it with one of his cameras.

"A portent," Sam said.

"Wolverhino don't like portents," Jaeger said, and they laughed, passing Jaeger's flask between them. Jaeger watched the cloud slowly shift and give way to the unseen winds that buffeted it, as the glinting stars gradually came into view, taking the sky for their own.

—

THE DEN

Night came, and then morning, with the two of them sheltering in a makeshift lean-to out of a copse of trees that Jaeger felt would give them at least enough of a warning if the Wolverhino sniffed them out and attacked.

They'd managed to recover their sleeping bags from the ruined Rover, hoping that the terrible smell would screen their scent from the beast, should it come barreling their way in the night hours.

"Man," Sam said. "I'm going to be smelling like that thing for years, now. My wife's gonna have me sleeping out in the back yard."

"It'll be okay," Jaeger said, after they ate some survival bars. "We're going to find its lair today."

"You think?" Sam asked.

"I've been triangulating it for the past three days," Jaeger said. "It's lairing somewhere in that woods there. At least for now, it is."

Then he carefully walked the perimeter of the glade, heading uphill, sniffing the air, trying to catch a fresh and unmistakable whiff of the Wolverhino.

"I always prefer stalking game," Jaeger said, while Sam filmed. "Some hunters like their tree stands and blinds, but to my mind, that's sniping, not proper hunting. The hunt is about the pursuit, not hanging around, waiting for the quarry to just blunder into your path."

"What about the Rover?" Sam asked.

"Only a tool," Jaeger said. "Flushing it out, as it were. I suppose I could have attempted what Jilton did and use the Rover as a blind, but it's just not my style."

The scent picked up, and Jaeger motioned for Sam to follow him through the fog, the two of them moving very quietly, with favorable wind. They made their way into the taiga yet again, this time following that track that Jaeger had intended to follow earlier, the one with the blood, before the attack on the Land Rover.

The two of them made their way through the dark conifers, with the benefit of the breaking of the day, instead of the rush to make their passage before dusk. Although precious little light found its way to the forest floor, there was still comfort Jaeger took in the idea that the sun was up there somewhere.

An hour into the woods, Jaeger kept to his tracking, finding fresher prints from the night before, by his estimation. And, to his delight, another clearing, where some heavy snow had fallen at some point.

In this place, there were beams of sunlight lancing inward at a thirty-degree angle, illuminating the fog. It was a beautiful moment, offset only by the monstrous musky stink of the Wolverhino, and the broken bones scattered about on the ground, indicated only by the abundant blood that had been spilled in the snow, and the shards of bone from where the creature had fed on them.

They made their way toward the edge of the tree line in this clearing, where there was a great hole in the snowy ground, screened by splintered trees and even more piles of broken and bloody bones. The reek from it was almost unbearable, made even Jaeger's eyes tear up.

"The den," Jaeger said, pointing, while Sam gagged a bit, keeping his camera aimed.

The hole had been dug, clawed from the frozen ground by the Wolverhino. The beast had taken great care to carve this place for itself in the ground.

"Is it in there?" Sam asked, and Jaeger steeled himself, walking closer to the lip of the den, with Beauty up and at the ready.

There was no way he was going to actually venture into the creature's den. That would have been suicidal, and whatever Jaeger was, he wasn't that.

Instead, he backed away from the den, taking up a position a couple dozen yards from the hole, motioning for Sam to back up with him. In the thicker snow in this clearing, it was hard to find the footing, but the two men managed, crunching some of the bones beneath their feet as they did so.

Jaeger was unsure if that was what had infuriated the Wolverhino, because the great beast roared and stormed out of its den with a great, snorting roar, vaulting beautifully in the motes of sunlight as it did so, like a whale breaching. It landed on the ground with a cataclysmic thump, and Jaeger raised Beauty to take his shot when the beast capered out into the fog, charging with its gamboling gait.

He pivoted his rifle in its direction, but the big beast, despite its behemoth-like bulk and the battles it had waged, remained shockingly spry. It moved swiftly out of sight, heading downhill toward some peat bogs, but not before Jaeger fired a shot with Beauty, the heavy shell catching the beast behind its shoulder.

"After it!" Jaeger said, stalking in its wake, careful not to twist an ankle in the fog-slicked and snowy ground.

The Wolverhino roared again, its voice echoing in the fog, but the beast was invisible, except for drips of its blood. To bring down something like this in a thick fog would be a marvelous accomplishment, although he doubted that Sam would be able to film much of it.

Tracking down through the taiga, toward the peat bog, following the trail of blood, senses keenly focused on his quarry, Jaeger paused, seeing the Wolverhino, luminous and menacing in the fog, backlit by the morning sun. It had turned to face them.

"Oh, I like this not at all," Jaeger said.

The thing gazed at them, panting, uncomprehending, enraged, the wind blowing at their backs, taking in their scents. In that moment, Jaeger felt sympathy for the monster, designed for his entertainment, and those like him. It did not ask to be made, and had no proper place in Nature. It did not belong on or in this or any world. It was a true monster, as portentous as the word, itself.

The Wolverhino dug its claws into the earth, ripping up great clods of peat, and tore uphill after Jaeger and Sam, its great, deadly, still-bloody horn curving elegantly atop its hideous face. It panted as it ran for them, great, broad snout venting steam, showing off its open mouth full of terrifying fangs—great, daggerlike canines and rows of incisors as big as dominoes. It was a mouth made for mayhem, capable of crunching down caribou bones with ease.

The rage of the thing was outmatched only by its considerable power. What moved on them was not so much a creature, as it was an elemental force of crashing hooves and clacking claws, of great, guttering breaths and that haunting, off-kilter grunt-roar that struck unforgettable fear into any who heard it, including Jaeger, himself.

Undeterred, Jaeger brought up Beauty and sighted her, mentally marking off the yards as the Wolver-hino charged them. With only one chambered round remaining in his rifle, and no time to reload or draw the Havilland, there was zero margin for error. Were he to miss, he would die as badly as Jilton and Aber-crombie had, as badly as Landon had. The Wolver-hino would run him down or split him in two with its ghastly horn. It would feast upon his flesh and bones.

Sam moved to his side, keeping his camera on the Wolverhino as it bounded for them, while Jaeger held his ground, every instinct honed for this moment, as he took careful aim once more. He forced himself to breathe easily, as the Wolverhino's claws tore up great blocks of podzol as it bore down on him, waiting for the thing to close to ten yards before finally pulling the trigger. The whole thing took only seconds, but, for Jaeger, it felt like his entire life.

Beauty fired, and the shot found its mark, catch-ing it right in the head, dropping the Wolverhino in mid-gallop, the beast striking the ground and sliding toward him, like a kind of bestial snowplow, upend-ing snow, soil and plant as it ground to a halt only a few feet before it reached Jaeger, who was reloading Beauty even as the thing slid toward him.

In that moment, there was only silence, the bellows of the breathing beast, breathing its last, and Jaeger's own thudding heartbeat.

"Damn, but that was one helluva shot, Jaeger," Sam said. "I caught it all."

"I appear to have done for the savage Wolverhino," Jaeger said, drawing his hunting knife and making his way up to the dying beast, its great heart still pounding, like muffled thunder.

It did not feel like a hunt in the moment, so much as it was a mercy killing. This thing did not ask to be created. It was the heaving hubris of Gaiacon made flesh, and Jaeger feared his own complicity in their plans. He could see their future hunting preserves, secreted away in distant wildernesses, protected by armed security. He could see clients flown in, flat eyes lit with fateful fervor, paying for the privilege of a chance to test their monied mettle against these cold and calculated creations.

The manufacture of monstrosity would become Gaiacon's lasting legacy, Jaeger was sure, and he was, in those last moments with the Wolverhino, an accessory to their crimes against nature. It was something he'd have to live with. Tilda would not have wanted this for him.

Jaeger steeled himself before the dying chimera. The Wolverino's eyes were already glazing over, blood tears in its eyes as Jaeger slipped past its massive, grasping clawed paws and buried the knife into its heart, laying his cheek against its thickly-furred chest as it breathed its last with a monstrous shudder.

"Rest in peace, Thunderer," Jaeger said.

"You want a shot with it, Jaeger?" Sam asked.

"I already took my shot, Sam," Jaeger said.

For the first time ever on the completion of a hunt, Jaeger did not pose in front of his kill. Although he had won, there was no prize for the taking, here.

—

THE INTERVIEW

He thought he could already detect the Gaiacon warden teams driving out from the gatehouse, judging from the sound of klaxons that he heard.

Jaeger's radio chirped, and it was Sloane Ketteridge.

"How did it go, Mr. Jaeger?" she asked, impossibly perky. "Besides losing Mr. James, I mean? We're all very broken up about what happened to him."

"We're still alive, if that's what you're asking, Ms. Ketteridge," Jaeger said.

"What did you think of the Wolverhino? Just tell me the first things that come to mind," Sloane asked.

Jaeger hunted for the right words. In fact, he was unsure what he should say. Gaiacon had invested enough that they would likely push forward with their project regardless of the input he provided. And yet, in that moment, there was also that opportunity for him to take some kind of stand. For the moment, the diplomat found the words.

"Formidable," Jaeger said. "Foul. The stink of it could peel paint off a wall."

"You don't like the smell?" Sloane asked, a ridiculous question. "Our design team felt like it would aid in tracking."

"Yes, I inferred that," Jaeger said, while Sam took photographs of the dead Wolverhino, covering it from every angle. "I didn't hear your team come in to recover Mr. James."

"They were hanging back until we were sure you've concluded your hunt, Mr. Jaeger, although Vitaly tells me they're on their way," Sloane said. "I just wanted to check in. We're happy that it was a successful hunt."

"I killed it," Jaeger said. Although it did not feel to him like it was truly a successful hunt. He had survived, and the Wolverhino was dead.

"Outstanding, Mr. Jaeger! On a 10-point scale, how would you rate your experience at the moment?" Sloane asked.

"Do we really have to do this now, Ms. Ketteridge?" Jaeger asked.

"We'd like to get at least a little on-site feedback, just for our records, while it's all still fresh in your mind," Sloane said.

Jaeger thought of what kind of epitaph he could leave for their corporate creation, what he, as one man, could possibly do to stop the mass production of this and other monsters like it. Tilda would have wanted him to. She would have called it out for what it was, and would have pitied the thing, tried to save it, somehow.

"It's undeniably fierce, if somewhat restive in its ranging. It's aggressive to the point of exhaustion, and devilishly territorial. I don't think it's particularly bright, but it is opportunistic, and has a wickedly good nose about it. It ferreted out our supplies in the Land Rover and sought to raid them, which is where poor Landon got into trouble. I'd recommend two- or three-jeep teams to hunt it effectively, with a shooter in each jeep, armed with high-caliber weapons. Oh, Mr. James managed to fire off several shots at the thing at point-blank range with a 9mm pistol and I think the bullets actually ricocheted, although it was hard to be sure."

"So, what I think I'm hearing is that you'd give this hunting experience an eight out of ten. Would that be fair, Mr. Jaeger?"

Jaeger glanced over at Sam, who looked at him in turn, having photographed his fill of the thing. It had never occurred to Jaeger to assign a number value to a hunt, could only feel a sense of diminishment in quantifying the experience in that manner.

"What's fair, Ms. Ketteridge?" Jaeger asked. "I don't think this was fair, by any means. Not for the Wolverhino, at any rate. If nothing else, if you were to throw an arbitrary number on it, for the singular novelty of the experience, I'd give it a five."

"A five?" Sloane said. "A five?"

"A five," Jaeger said.

"What would we have done better, Mr. Jaeger?" Sloane asked.

This was Tilda's moment. It was her voice inside him, his memory of her.

"Beyond never making the thing at all?" Jaeger asked. "That's the only way you could have improved the experience."

Sloane was quiet on the line a moment, and Jaeger could almost see her deciding what to say next, in her lovely home office, or wherever it was she worked.

"I'm afraid that's beyond consideration, Mr. Jaeger," Sloane said. "The project will go forward."

"I know," Jaeger said, watching Sam take down his gear, stowing it. Their eyes met, an unspoken understanding between them.

"Perfectly said, Mr. Jaeger. Glad we have an understanding. And, congratulations on being the very first person to bag a Wolverhino. You've made history today," Sloane said. "You may be interested to know that we have an Eelephant bull available for hunting. There's also a Polarctic Sealbear, as well as a Honey Badgerconda ready for field-testing. Prey for the Future, Mr. Jaeger, just as we promised."

"I intend to, Ms. Ketteridge," Jaeger said, knowing the pun would pass unnoticed, although Tilda would snared it in a heartbeat. He hung up and made sure to turn off the ringer for his phone, while Sam looked on.

"Honey Badgercondas, Polarctic Sealbears, Eelephants, Mr. Henry," Jaeger said. "More prize chimeras in Gaiacon's dread menagerie."

"They do love their market research at Gaiacon," Sam said.

"It's the price of admission, apparently," Jaeger said, as they headed back into the glade, which was thick with fog. He paused a moment, listening. The ravens could be heard squawking. Jaeger dug out his flask, unscrewed the lid.

"Where are you gonna put your trophy?" Sam asked.

"Right here seems fine," Jaeger said. "I'm going to leave it for the birds."

Sam seemed surprised, smiled to himself, shaking his head, chuckling.

"Wolverhino don't care about market research," Sam said, mimicking Landon's butchered pronunciation of it.

"Wolverhino don't care one bit," Jaeger said, smiling sadly, and the two shared a couple of drinks from Jaeger's flask, after pouring out a dram for poor Landon. As the distant Gaiaconvoy made its way toward them, the two men watched the ravens gather in the trees, anticipating yet another great feast.

—

FINIS

ACKNOWLEDGMENTS

I would like to thank all of my readers, who offered their time, attention, and opinions to the writing and revision of this novella. I would also like to thank Christine Marie Scott of Clever Crow Design Studio in Pittsburgh for her wonderful cover art and her invaluable assistance with the layout of these pages.

ABOUT THE AUTHOR

Dean Vale lives and breathes Science Fiction at all hours in a 1920s brownstone, where he conjures up progressively more dystopian and utopian visions for the future of humankind.

DEANVALE.COM

ALSO BY DEAN VALE

Farther

NOSETOUCH PRESS

Nosetouch Press is an independent book publisher
tandemly-based in Chicago and Pittsburgh.
We are dedicated to bringing some of today's most
energizing fiction to readers around the world.

Our commitment to classic book design in a digital
environment brings an innovative and authentic
approach to the traditions of literary excellence.

*The Nose Knows™

NOSETOUCHPRESS.COM

Horror | Science Fiction | Fantasy | Mystery | Supernatural